"Can I speak to Dawn, please?" The girl's voice on the other end of the receiver sounded quivery and familiar.

"This is Dawn. Who's this?"

"I-it's me—Marlee Hodges."

For no reason, Dawn's heart skipped a beat. "Hi. How are you? Is everything all right?"

"No." Marlee's voice wavered.

Dawn clutched the receiver so tightly that her fingers hurt. "What's wrong?"

"I'm back in the hospital and I'm scared. Please, come see me, Dawn. Please."

SO MUCH
TO LIVE FOR

Lurlene McDaniel

SCHOLASTIC INC.

New York Toronto London Auckland Sydney
Mexico City New Delhi Hong Kong Buenos Aires

I would like to especially thank the campers of Camp Horizon, Nashville, Tennessee,
for their willingness to share.
And also, thanks to Valerie and Linda.

ISBN 0-439-69214-8

12 11 10 9 8 7 6 5 4 3 2 1   5 6 7 8 9 0/0

Printed in the U.S.A.   01

First Scholastic printing, January 2005

Cover photo and design by Michael Petty
Petty Productions

One

"ARE you scared?"

Dawn Rochelle glanced toward her brother Rob and considered his question for a moment before answering. "Well, maybe just a little."

"I think you'll do fine," he told her as he pushed his foot on the accelerator and passed a slow-moving truck on the winding country road. "Besides you've been to camp before, so what's to be scared about?"

"Well, for one thing I've never been a counselor before. It'll be different than just being a regular camper."

"That's why you're going up early—so you can go through training." Rob reached over and slugged his sister's shoulder affectionately. "Come on. Where's that old Rochelle enthusiasm? Think of all the fun you're going to have. Katie says you'll be the best counselor-in-training in the group."

Dawn gave him a bright smile, one far more courageous than she felt. How had she ever let Joan Clark at the clinic talk her into becoming a CIT at cancer camp this summer?

Dawn thought back to the day she'd come into the clinic for routine blood work and Joan had corralled her in her office. There, she'd explained how important she felt it was to have teens who'd had cancer work with kids who were also cancer victims. It was one way to show the younger kids that it was possible to survive cancer and live a normal life.

"But why me?" Dawn had asked Joan. "I wasn't even planning on going to camp this year. I promised my friend Rhonda that I'd work at her uncle's ice cream parlor this summer."

In truth, at 15, Dawn was tired of the whole business of leukemia. After all, she'd been through a lot since her diagnosis—hospitalization, months of chemotherapy and sickness, remission, relapse and finally, a bone marrow transplant from her brother. Since then, her blood work had been free of cancer cells, but she knew that there were no guarantees. Her doctors wanted her marrow working for several years before they pronounced her cured.

But Joan had shrugged off Dawn's comment. "I'm asking you because you've been through so much with your disease, and because you seemed to have such a good time at camp."

"Oh, I did. It's a wonderful place for kids with cancer. It helps them know that they're not alone, that there are others who are going through the same things. The first time I went, I thought it was the most wonderful place in the world."

But the first time Dawn had gone to camp her friend Sandy Chandler had gone too and they'd met Mike and Greg. Now Mike was off in college, Greg had moved, and Sandy—well, Sandy was gone forever.

"There'll be other CITs your age," Joan offered. "Six of you. You'll go in three days early for training with the rest of the staff. I think you're perfect for the job, Dawn. Please say you'll do it."

The memory of Joan's office faded as Dawn stared out the car window and watched as they passed by the wooded Ohio countryside.

"It's too bad Katie couldn't come with

us today," she said to Rob, sighing a mock sigh. She watched as the tips of Rob's ears turned red and a funny little smile tugged at his mouth. "Don't forget, Rob, if it hadn't been for me, you'd never have met Katie."

"An event that will forever put me in your debt," Rob said, lifting one hand off the steering wheel in a little salute.

Katie had been the nurse assigned to Dawn's case during her transplant procedure. Dawn adored her and hoped that she and Rob would be happy together. Rob had had a tough time with girls lately. Just before her bone marrow transplant he had broken up with his fiancée, Darcy, and he was just now getting over it. "So I guess you'll be seeing her a lot this summer, huh?"

"Why do you think I've decided to take a job in Columbus instead of staying at the university and finding summer work there?" Rob asked, his eyes twinkling.

Dawn tapped the side of her forehead, pretending that she was concentrating hard. "Do I get a prize for the right answer?"

Rob flashed her a grin. "*You* can have anything you want from me, little sister."

Dawn returned his smile. But she

thought that even if a magic genie appeared to grant her a wish, she wasn't sure what it would be at the moment. Her feelings were a jumble of anticipation, apprehension and wistfulness as Rob turned into the familiar rutted roadway that led to the main buildings of the camp area. Trees wore the richly hued shades of June green and their leafy arms stretched over the roadway like a canopy. Dawn rolled down the window and sniffed the sweet, fragrant air.

Rob slowed the car to a crawl. "Does it bring back memories?" he asked.

"How did you know?"

"We're joined by bone marrow, remember?"

Dawn laid her head against the car seat headrest and stared upward through the windshield at the flecks of blue sky between tree branches. "Yes, it brings back lots of memories."

Rob turned off the engine. "Why don't you wait a few minutes before I drop you off at the main building?"

"I'll be late for the first meeting."

"So what? Tell me what's on your mind."

"I'm not sure I can explain it."

"Try. Are you sorry you came?"

"No. I'm glad to help out. It's just hard

coming back, that's all."

"Why?"

Dawn searched for a way to put her mixed-up feelings into words, a way to make him understand the turmoil she felt. "I-I'm never sure who'll be back from the year before."

"There are plenty of reasons kids stop coming to camp, Dawn."

She turned her head so that she could see his face. "This is *cancer* camp, Rob. When kids stop coming, you don't always know why. Sometimes it's because they move or get busy with something else. And sometimes, it's because they...." She let the sentence trail, unable to say the word.

"It's because they die," Rob finished for her. "Like Sandy did. I'm sorry, Squirt."

A film of tears formed over Dawn's eyes and she turned her head quickly. She didn't want to go into a meeting with red puffy eyes and besides, Sandy had been gone for a long time. She should be over it by now. "She was my very best friend. I still miss her, you know?"

Rob placed his hand on her shoulder and gave a gentle squeeze. "I know and I hate to see you hurting over it."

"Hurting is what happens when you

make friends with someone who has cancer," Dawn explained with a sigh. "It's just hard watching people go away when they have so much to live for. It's not fair to have life taken away from kids who have dreams and plans and stuff."

Her voice threatened to break, so she stopped talking and thought back to Sandy. Sandy had died in a clinic in Mexico far away from her home in West Virginia. She never even got to finish seventh grade, or see her sister and two brothers again, or kiss the boy she thought she loved.

After Sandy's death, Sandy's parents had sent Dawn a cardboard box filled with special items Sandy had wanted Dawn to have. She used to sort through them often. But every time she did, she cried so hard she had trouble stopping. Finally, she'd had to store the box in her attic. She couldn't recall the last time she'd gone through it, but she could remember every single item with crystal clarity. The combs Sandy had worn in her baby fine blond hair. The craft projects from their days together in the hospital and at camp. Sandy's diary.

A tear trickled down Dawn's cheek and she wiped it with the back of her hand.

"Are you okay?" Rob's voice sounded

alarmed when he asked her.

Dawn sniffed and dragged her thoughts back into the present. "Sure. I just got a little weepy thinking about Sandy and all."

Rob smoothed her red-brown hair which now had grown past her shoulders. "Should I go ahead and take you to the main hall?"

"Take me to my cabin first so I can dump my stuff."

Rob re-started the car and headed up the roadway. "I think you're going to have a great time," he told her cheerfully. "Who knows? Maybe you'll make some really cool new friends."

"Maybe," Dawn said, without believing it. Deep down, she wasn't sure she wanted to make new friends with kids who had cancer. It hurt too bad when she lost them.

All she really wanted to do was fulfill her commitment to the CIT program and go back home and work in the ice cream parlor with Rhonda. When school started in the fall, she'd be a sophomore in a brand new school where most people didn't know her. No one would think of her as the girl who has cancer. She could make lots of friends with kids who were normal and didn't have to face the idea of maybe dying before they ever had a chance to live.

Two

"SORRY I'm late," Dawn said as she hurried into the main hall where campers met, ate and held activities on rainy days. A small group of people sat around one of the wooden dining tables. Dawn quickly counted twelve adults and five kids about her age. She recognized some of the faces from the last time she was at camp.

At one end of the table Dr. Ben stood, wearing his familiar baseball hat. "Dawn, good to see you!" He motioned her toward him. "This is Dawn Rochelle, everybody." He held out his hand, but before she could shake it, he withdrew it.

"Wait a minute," he said. "You haven't got an electric joy buzzer hidden in your palm, have you? I mean, I remember the last time I saw you. It took me an hour to clean off the raw eggs and flour." His eyes held a teasing glimmer behind the thick lenses of his glasses.

Dawn blushed and laughed along with the others. It was camp tradition to play a special prank on Dr. Ben. Fortunately, he was a good sport and seemed to actually enjoy the pranks. She figured he'd never forget the time she, Sandy, Mike and Greg had stolen his underwear, sewn flowers on a pair and run them up the flagpole.

She held up her hands, showing them to be empty. "No. I'm clean."

"Well, okay then," he said, grasping her hand and shaking it firmly. Then he pointed to an empty chair. She sat down as he began to speak.

"These packets will explain our overall philosophy, as well as give a thumb-nail sketch of day-to-day activities." He passed around colored folders, filled with sheaves of paper.

Dawn took hers and leafed through the sheets. She wondered again if she should have taken the job. There seemed to be so much to learn.

"Don't panic, folks," Dr. Ben said, almost as if reading Dawn's thoughts. "We've got three days to sort through this stuff and get prepared. Each cabin will be assigned one medical staff member, one CIT and six campers."

From the other side of the table, a woman she remembered as Gail motioned to Dawn and mouthed, "We're together." Dawn smiled and started to go back to reading her folder. Then she noticed a boy sitting beside Gail. He was slim and blond, blue-eyed too. But it wasn't simply his good looks that kept her glancing at him. Something about him looked familiar.

Impossible, she told herself. She recognized most of the people around the table, but she was certain she'd never met him before. Yet she couldn't shake the nagging feeling that she somehow knew him too.

"...start with the bonfire," Dr. Ben was saying. His words jerked Dawn back into the flow of the meeting. *The bonfire.* Dawn knew it was the emotional highlight of every camp session. At the bonfire the campers returned ashes from the previous year's fire and removed ashes from the present year's to take home with them. Returning the ashes was a symbol that they had survived to come back to camp another year.

The ceremony she and Sandy had participated in together leapt to life in her memory as if it were yesterday. She remembered Sandy telling her, "Let's be sure to be here next year." And her own determined reply, "I'll be back." But Sandy didn't return and even now, two years later, recalling their broken promise made Dawn feel helpless and embittered.

Dr. Ben's voice cut through her thoughts. "We'll need people to play the Indians, of course. They'll man the canoe and bring the lighted torches across the lake. Tom, you did it last year. How about you and Gail?"

Dawn turned to see Tom, but her gaze tripped over the blond boy on the far side of the table. His eyes held hers and he offered a smile. She felt her cheeks grow red, not only because he'd caught her staring at him, but because his smile and face looked so hauntingly familiar.

"...you CITs will be leading all the songs." Once again, Dawn had to force herself to pay attention to what Dr. Ben was saying.

"But I can't sing," one girl wailed.

"Neither can I," one of the boys echoed.

"So what?" Dr. Ben said with a grin. "It's

a dirty job, but someone has to do it."

"Are we getting all the dirty work?" a girl Dawn knew as Shelly asked Dr. Ben suspiciously.

"Would I give you kids *all* the dirty work?" Dr. Ben asked them in wide-eyed innocence.

The CITs exchanged glances, then chimed, "Yes!"

"You're right," Dr. Ben said. "But rank has its privileges."

Several of them wadded up scrap paper and threw it at Dr. Ben.

"Testy, aren't they?" Dr. Ben asked of the other staff members, most of whom were doubled over in laughter.

"What other little surprises have you got for us?" another counselor asked.

"Cabin inspections."

"But kids *hate* cleaning up the cabins."

"Naturally. That's why you get to make sure they do it."

"Unfair. They'll hate us," one of the CITs answered.

Dr. Ben chuckled. "I know." He cleared his throat amidst good-natured jeering from the CITs. "Also, you'll be responsible for assisting in our special events—like Fifties Night, State Fair Day, Indian Day and my personal favorite— the Junior Olympics."

Dawn brightened, remembering the events from the Olympics she and Sandy had been a part of two years before. Together, they'd had so much fun, and simply thinking back to the day brought back the sound of Sandy's lilting laughter. Dr. Ben's voice intruded into her memories. "This year we'll be adding a new event, Tug-of-War Over the Biggest Mudhole We Can Make."

A cheer went up from the CITs. "Our chance to get even, guys," Tony shouted.

"You'll eat dirt, Dr. Ben," Dawn heard herself call out.

The camp director let everyone joke good-naturedly for a few minutes, then took control of the briefing once more. "The important thing for you CITs is to be available to the campers. For lots of them, this will be their first time away from home, certainly their first time away from the medical regime. Most will be on their drug protocols, chemo pills, and pain medications. We'll be responsible for dispensing them." He gestured toward the adult medical personnel.

"But for the most part, these kids will

look to you CITs for help. I plan to break into small groups each day for rap sessions—you know, a time set aside for sharing thoughts and feelings. You CITs will be especially valuable in these sessions, because I think kids will tell other kids things they might not share with adults."

The mood in the room had sobered. Dawn realized that despite all the teasing and joking, no one could forget these were not ordinary, typical campers away from home for a few weeks of fun. These were kids with cancer, whose time at camp might be the only fun they had all year. Dawn knew their world. It was a world of constant pain, spinal taps, bloodwork, nausea from chemo and radiation therapy. A world of hospitals, labs, clinics, and for some—like Sandy—a cemetery.

*   *   *   *   *

After lunch, Dr. Ben told everybody to take a break and meet back in the hall at 4:00. Dawn was grateful for the chance to escape outdoors and she took off alone toward the lake. She rounded a bend and heard someone call her name from behind. She turned to see the blond boy from the dining hall jogging toward her.

He stopped in front of her. "Hi," he said, his smile open and friendly. "I've been wanting to talk to you."

His accent was softly southern, another prick against her memory. "I—I feel as if we've met," she said, hoping to explain the weird way she knew she must be acting. "But we haven't. Have we?"

"In a way," the boy said. "You missed the formal introductions at Dr. Ben's meeting since you were late. I'm Brent Chandler. You knew my sister, Sandy."

Three

DAWN'S breath caught and she stared up at him. Of course! Now she saw it so clearly. His resemblance to Sandy was striking. "I—I didn't recognize...."

"That's all right," he said with a smile. "I wouldn't have expected you to know me."

"Sandy talked about her family when we were in the hospital, but that was over two years ago."

"Well, you were *all* she talked about after she came home that time. It was 'Dawn this' and 'Dawn that'—I swear she almost drove us crazy waiting for the mailman to bring your letters."

Dawn felt goose bumps break out on her arms. It was weird being so close to someone who was Sandy's flesh and blood. "You all must miss her a lot."

"I was 15 when she died." His blue eyes

clouded momentarily. "It was a hard time for all of us. Especially for Dad. Sandy was so special to him. I don't think he'll ever get over losing her."

"What are your folks doing now?"

"Oh, Dad's a foreman at the mines and Mama works in a department store. 'Course, my little sister Jennifer's still at home with them. I graduated from high school a few weeks ago and plan to go to West Virginia Tech in the fall. I think I'd like to be a doctor."

Dawn shook her head with a smile. Brent sounded so much like Sandy. Sandy was always giving her volumes of information to answer one simple question. "Well, I don't want to have anything to do with medicine ever again," she insisted. "Taking an aspirin is about the strongest medicine I hope to swallow. And if somebody tries to take any more of my blood, I'll punch him out!"

Brent laughed. "That's how Sandy felt. She took fistfuls of pills that made her sick. But she *had* to take them, 'cause the doctors said it was the only way to kill her cancer."

"She and I used to wonder if the cure wasn't worse than the disease." Dawn told him, anxious to talk about her friend. "By the way, I kept all the stuff of hers your parents sent me. I used to go through it." She decided against telling him that she didn't do it anymore, that it hurt her heart too much to touch all of Sandy's possessions. "Sandy was my best friend," Dawn added, "and even now, though I have other friends, no one understood me like she did."

"I guess it's 'cause of the things you shared."

"I guess so."

A silence fell between them and Dawn felt waves of sadness wash over her. Perhaps it was the sight of the cabins where she and Sandy had lain awake talking half the night. Or maybe it was the scent of the surrounding woods bringing back images of the two of them walking hand in hand with Greg and Mike. She felt a sudden urge to cry.

"Now I've gone and depressed you, haven't I?" Brent asked in his slow southern drawl. "I surely didn't mean to do that."

Dawn shook off her sadness. "No way. One thing I refuse to be is depressed, especially not after what I've been through with my cancer." She told him about her relapse and transplant.

"That's some story," he said softly when she finished. "I sometimes wonder if things might have been different for Sandy if my Dad hadn't decided to take her down to Mexico for that experimental therapy instead of going back to the hospital the way Dr. Sinclair wanted her to."

"She wrote me from Mexico and said that she wasn't sick like when she was on chemo."

"Yeah, but they didn't cure her did they? I'll always wonder if maybe she'd have been better off if she'd gone back to Columbus. Maybe a bone marrow transplant would have helped her like it did you."

"Maybe," Dawn said thoughtfully. "But even though the treatment's working in me, I still worry every time I go in for a check-up. What if it stops working?"

"Well, you sure look healthy right now," Brent told her.

She felt her pulse flutter and self-consciously, changed the subject. "Umm, I was headed down to the lake. Do you want to come?"

"Sure. I need to get to know this place like the back of my hand so that I can't get lost. You others have an advantage because you've been here before."

They started down the trail. Dawn tugged at a leaf from an overhanging tree and inspected its texture as they walked. "This is the third time I've come, but the first time as a CIT."

"I've been looking forward to it for months."

"I'm glad we've got a few days of training. I hope the campers will listen to what I tell them. And I hope they don't think I'm trying to be bossy." Dawn glanced over at Brent thoughtfully. Then she asked, "How come you get to be a CIT? I thought they only used kids who have had cancer."

"I guess they figured that, because of Sandy, I was pretty close to the disease," he answered. "Besides, there's another camp right after this one for the brothers and sisters of kids who have had cancer and I'm going to work as a counselor for that camp too."

"Really? Why do brothers and sisters need a special camp? Cancer's not happening to them."

"You better believe it's happening to us! When I first heard about Sandy, I got so angry that I smashed my foot right through my bedroom door. I just kept wondering, 'Why my sister?' I still don't have the answer to that one."

Dawn understood. Hadn't she often wondered why she had lived and Sandy had died? Was it like a game of eeny-meeny-miny-moe, where people got tossed away because they were standing in the wrong line?

She crumpled the leaf. "Well, the living part's not so easy either," she told Brent. "You feel divided in half. Part of you is trying to deal with all these problems from having cancer, and part of you is trying to a be regular person. For me, the hardest part was trying to fit back into school and all. My teachers acted afraid *for* me, and my friends acted weird—like I was contagious or something."

"Yeah, Sandy's so-called friends made me mad," he replied. "They ignored her or treated her like she was a freak. I know now they were just scared. But at the time, I could've killed them."

"You've got to admit, cancer's pretty scary. Everybody's afraid of it. They can't help thinking, 'What if cancer happens to me?'"

Brent stopped. Sunlight breaking through the overhead tree branches speckled his head and shoulders with leaf patterns. "You know what I sometimes feel really bad about?" She shook her head to his question.

"Even though I was real sorry for Sandy, I was glad it wasn't happening to me. I used to feel pretty guilty because I didn't want to trade places with her."

"Who would?"

"But maybe I'd have done better with it than she did."

"Don't feel bad. I used to wish it wasn't happening to me. But then I couldn't wish it on somebody else either—that wouldn't have been right."

"Nobody gets to pick what happens to him, I guess," Brent observed, then started walking again.

"Sometimes I was scared for my family," Dawn admitted, kicking a loose pebble along the footpath. "I was afraid Rob might have to drop out of college because the hospital and operation cost so much."

"I actually got mad at Sandy because of the costs," Brent said, shaking his head. "We never had much in the first place and then when she got sick, Dad took double shifts and Mom worked two jobs. And when she went off to Mexico, well, I kept picturing her laying around by a pool and getting a suntan."

"But that's not the way it was," Dawn said, in defense of her friend. "She was lonesome and pretty sad most of the time."

"I know that now. And when she went off, I never dreamed she'd come home in a coffin." His words made Dawn shiver. At least her last vision of Sandy had been of hugging her good-bye at camp.

"Your brother was lucky," Brent told her. "He actually got to *do* something for you by donating his marrow. I never got to do anything for Sandy. So I guess that's why I wanted to work at this camp so bad. It makes me feel like I'm doing something for her."

"Do you have a special job?" she asked. By now they had walked out of the woods and were standing on a sand-packed stretch of beach that led down to the lapping waters of the brilliant blue lake.

"I'm in charge of the sports activities." He gazed toward a long wooden pier that jutted out into the water. "Swimming and diving are my favorites."

"I can't dive at all," Dawn admitted. "Sandy tried to teach me in the pool, but I was hopeless."

"I can teach you," he said looking her

over. "Who do you think taught Sandy?"

She imagined Brent and Sandy together, their blond hair reflecting the sun. Trouble was, Brent looked as he did now—grown—and in her mind's eye, Sandy was still thirteen. She knew how much she had changed in two years. How much would her friend have changed by now if she had lived?

"I always loved the water," Brent said. "Someday I hope I can live by the ocean."

Dawn considered his dream. It had been a long time since she thought that far into the future. The most she could muster were thoughts about being a sophomore in high school. And even that seemed a long way off. Here Brent was planning on college, on a career, on living by the sea. "I hope you get it all, Brent," she said.

"I hope you get everything you want too, Dawn."

She told him thanks and meant it. But at the moment she had absolutely no idea what her future might be. No idea at all.

Four

AS the three days of training passed, Dawn grew more confident about being a CIT. As the first day of camp approached, she and Gail aired out the cabin, made large "welcome" signs and crepe paper banners and strung them inside and outside of the cabin.

Dr. Ben's briefings and brainstorming sessions turned up wonderful ideas. "We could make a game of cabin inspection," Theresa suggested. "We'll take turns giving out a daily award for the neatest cabin."

"Why don't we make the reward extra food?" Tony asked. "I know when I was taking some of those chemo medications they made me so hungry I could have eaten the paint off the walls."

"Good idea," Dr. Ben said. "We'll give the cabin that wins the most inspections a pizza party on the last night."

On the day the campers were scheduled to arrive, Dr. Ben asked, "Are we ready?" and the counselors answered with a resounding "Yes!"

Dawn was still nervous but she was excited too. She really wanted to show the campers in her group a very special time and had been trying to think of an extra something she could do for them.

Right after lunch, an idea came to her. She grabbed Brent by the hand and whispered, "Come on with me."

She led him into a large meadow awash with colorful wildflowers and dancing butterflies. The high grass tickled her bare legs as she walked through it. "What are we going to do?" Brent wanted to know.

"Pick flowers," she told him. "I think it'd be nice to put a bouquet and a name card on every bunk as a special welcome. I remember the first time I came to camp. If Sandy hadn't been there, I would have fainted from fright."

Brent grinned. "Her bag was packed a week before she left 'cause she couldn't wait to get here and be with you."

Dawn felt her chest hurt with longing. Would she ever stop missing her Sandy?

"We'd better hurry," she told Brent stooping to pull up a clump of wild daisies.

He helped her and in no time they'd gathered an armful of tiny, bright colored flowers. Back at the cabin, Dawn carefully separated them out and tied ribbon loosely around the stems to form a cluster. Brent placed a spray on each pillow while Dawn made name cards sprinkled with glitter.

When everything was ready, she gazed around the cabin with pride and asked, "The place looks pretty good, doesn't it? Once all the bare mattresses are covered, it'll look like a home." Her own bed was neatly made, spread with a patchwork quilt her grandmother had made years before.

"Looks super," he told her, wandering over to her bunk. "Is this yours?" He picked up her favorite teddy bear, Mr. Ruggers.

Dawn felt herself blush. *Great*, she thought. *A teddy bear on the bunk of the CIT really makes a mature statement.* Brent probably thought she was a silly little kid for lugging along her dog-eared bear.

"Oh, it's just something to make the younger kids feel more at home," she said as casually as possible. "The girls in my cabin are 10, 11 and 12. Except for Marlee, the oldest—she's 13. I—um—sort of thought it might make them feel more at ease."

"He looks like he's been through a war," Brent said as he studied the scruffy old bear. One glass eye was missing and his red, felt tongue had been partially torn off.

That's exactly what he has been through, Dawn thought, remembering how she'd used him in her imaging therapy to fight off ugly cancer cells. Brent handed her the old bear. "Sandy drew me a poster with him in it. I guess I should throw him away. He does look pretty ratty." She gave a self-conscious shrug and tossed the bear back onto the quilt.

In the distance, she heard the camp bell ringing. "That's our signal," she said. "I guess the first campers are here."

"Then let's go get 'em!" Brent answered with a grin. He hooked his arm through hers and they hurried to the assembly hall.

Inside the hall, Dawn could scarcely believe the bedlam. Campers and all their belongings were piled in every open space. Those who'd attended camp before were running around hugging and shouting at old friends. Those who'd never come looked scared or lost.

A familiar feeling crept over her as she watched the activity and remembered how excited she was about seeing Sandy after months of being separated from each other. When they'd seen each other they'd run and squealed and hugged and...Dawn caught herself before the memory became too painful and pushed it aside.

Over at the registration table, each camper was receiving a packet that held, among other things, cabin assignments. There were large signs along the walls with cabin numbers on them. Dawn waited beneath her sign, welcoming each girl as she came over. Within the next 30 minutes she'd collected five of her six campers.

Fran and Cindy wore scarves, so she guessed they were bald from chemo. Esther looked bloated, heavy with retained fluids, a side effect of certain medications. Val looked perfectly fine and Paige, the youngest, had only one arm—a result of bone cancer. Yet each of the girls seemed happy and excited about being at camp.

It didn't take the girls long to grow squirmy. "Can we go to our cabin now?" Esther asked.

"I was waiting on Marlee," Dawn shouted

above the noise. "Does anyone know what she looks like?"

The girls shook their heads in unison. "She's a civilian," Val announced, using the camp term for those who'd never attended camp before. "I would have remembered a girl named Marlee if she'd been here before."

"Have you?" Dawn asked.

"I've been coming since I was eight," Val answered. "Don't you remember me? I remember seeing you here." Dawn studied Val's upturned face and thought hard. "I was just a kid before," Val added. "And last year I was wearing a wig, but I'm in remission now."

I was just a kid before. The innocence of her remark caught Dawn off-guard and caused a small lump to rise up in her throat. Val was *still* a kid. All of them were.

Dawn cleared her throat and shouted over the racket, "Look, why don't I take you down to our cabin and let you start making up your bunks and stashing your stuff. I'll come back and wait for Marlee."

The girls grabbed their belongings and followed her outside and down the trail, chattering all the way. Hearing them talk, knowing the plans the staff had for them, gave her a sense of calm. She was suddenly glad she'd agreed to be a CIT.

"Let's sing!" Dawn cried, and began chanting, "Heigh ho, heigh ho, It's off to camp we go...." Behind her, the girls joined in and by the time they arrived at the cabin, their voices filled up the woods. They tramped up onto the porch. Dawn flung open the screen door and led them inside, where she stopped stark still, the words of the song dying on her lips.

The cabin looked like a storm had passed through. The signs hung down, the banners fluttered unstrung from the rafters, flowers lay in scattered heaps. Dawn's bedcovers were in a jumble on the floor, her pillow and Mr. Ruggers were in a heap in a corner. A girl was stretched out on Dawn's now bare mattress, nonchalantly reading a magazine, her feet propped up on a leather suitcase.

She lowered the magazine, studied the group and said, "I'm Marlee. I found this cabin without any dumb help from you. And that stupid song you're singing is getting on my nerves."

Five

FOR an instant, Dawn was speechless. Confusion and anger tumbled through her with lightning speed. Behind her, five wide-eyed girls crowded, waiting to see what she would do.

Where's Gail? she wondered frantically. Then she recalled seeing her back in the hall reassuring some anxious parents. Gail wasn't going to be here any time soon to help her handle this. Dawn swallowed hard.

"That's my bed," she said, trying to keep her voice even and controlled.

Marlee, didn't look up. "Oh, really?"

"Your name tag is over there." Dawn pointed to a bunk across the room. Marlee's nametag and flowers littered the floor.

"I saw it, but I like this bunk better."

Dawn took a deep breath, trying to calm

her racing heart and boiling emotions. She stepped over her bedcovers wadded on the floor. "Well you can't have this bunk. It's mine."

Marlee glared up at her. Struck by the glittering hostility in Marlee's eyes, Dawn almost backed off. But some instinct told her that if she lost this battle, she'd lose the confidence of the others and her authority to be a counselor.

"I want this bunk." Marlee said.

"Well, you can't have it."

"What are you going to do about it?" Marlee's chin butted defiantly.

Dawn took a long hard look at her challenger. Marlee was thin and lean. She was partially bald with wispy tufts of hair standing straight out. Her eyes were green and one seemed fixed and staring. She looked more pitiful than mean, but Dawn refused to overlook her attitude. "I've got 20 pounds on you, Marlee. Now get off my bed before I throw you off."

"You better not try." Marlee sounded tough, but Dawn saw her gaze waver and a look of surprise cross her face.

"Don't push me," Dawn warned.

"I have cancer," Marlee said, tossing the words haughtily.

"Who in this room doesn't?" Dawn challenged as she gestured to the girls pressed together in a huddle in back of her.

Marlee eyed her skeptically. "You don't look like you have it."

"You should have seen me when I was on chemo. I looked pretty grim."

"We all have cancer," one of the girls said. "You can't come to this camp unless you have cancer."

"Who asked you?" Marlee snapped. "I didn't want to come to this stupid place anyway."

"Then why did you?" Fran asked.

"None of your business, birdbrain." Marlee jumped off the mattress and hauled up her suitcase. It was so large and heavy that she staggered. Dawn's arm shot out to help, but Marlee gave her a warning look that said, *Don't touch.*

Marlee dragged the suitcase across the wooden floor to her assigned bunk. "Go ahead, take your dumb old bed. Who cares? Just leave me alone and don't tell me what to do."

Dawn took a deep breath, her knees shaking. But she said, "Wait, Marlee. You trashed my bed, I expect you to make it for me."

"In your dreams!"

"I mean it, Marlee." She stepped toward the girl. "Make yours and then mine."

"What are you going to do if I don't? Send me home?"

Rats, Dawn thought. Maybe she shouldn't have challenged her. "I'm not sending you home—you're here to stay."

"Fine," Marlee said, jerking Dawn's bedding up off the floor. "This stinks! I'm stuck here with a bunch of losers."

Dawn ignored her and turned to the other girls. "All right. Let's get those beds made. We've got to be back in the mess hall for supper in an hour."

The girls scurried off to their respective beds and began unpacking while Dawn walked calmly into the bathroom and shut the door. Once inside, she sagged over the sink and let her breath out in one long slow motion. Her hands were trembling and sweat was running between her shoulder blades.

"Just when I was starting to think this was a good idea," she muttered at her reflection in the mirror. Well, she'd won the first round. But if Marlee was going to continue to be such a brat, then this would surely be the longest week in Dawn's life.

* * * * *

Back in the hall for supper, Dawn told Gail what had happened. "Sounds like she's a pretty angry girl," Gail said. "We'll have to watch her closely. Go tell Dr. Ben."

She wasn't able to speak to Dr. Ben until after the campers had played several get-acquainted games and headed down to the lake for the bonfire ritual. On the trail, she quickly spilled her story to Dr. Ben. "Marlee Hodges," he said, flipping through his clipboard, until he found his mini-profile on her. "She's from Columbus—your hometown."

"Terrific," Dawn said sourly.

"Let's see—she has non-Hodgkin's lymphoma—that's cancer that causes tumors to grow on internal organs. She's had two operations to remove tumors and it says here that she lost an eye."

"She did?"

"Her left eye is artificial. She's still taking chemo, so coming to camp may be a bit overwhelming. Her hostility can be a cover up for fear."

"But she acted so hateful."

Dr. Ben studied his clipboard again. "It

41

says that both her parents are deceased and that she lives with her grandmother on her father's side. She's Marlee's legal guardian."

Dawn thought back to all the times her parents and Rob had helped her through her illness. She knew she couldn't have made it so far without them. But Marlee was partially blind and had no parents. She began to feel sorry for the girl. "How should I treat her?"

"Sounds to me like you did just fine."

"I did?"

"She's probably pretty scared and angry. You were 13 when you were diagnosed, weren't you?" he asked.

She nodded.

"Think back to how overwhelmed you felt. Maybe she'll open up in rap sessions," he suggested. "Let me know how it goes."

By then they'd arrived at the lake and the campers were settling around a pyramid of logs and sticks. Dawn quickly took a place between Val and Esther. Directly across from her she saw Brent with several young boys huddled around him. He waved and smiled and she smiled back. But her mind was still mulling over the problem of Marlee.

The sun set in a red ball and the sky filled with brilliant hues of red, lavender and violet. The group grew quiet. From the middle of the lake, a canoe began its advance through the darkening waters. Soon two Indians stepped onto the shore, each carrying lighted torches. Dawn listened as Dr. Ben invited the campers to empty their ashes on the fire.

Slowly, campers filed forward, shaking out the contents of boxes and bags. She also stepped forward. Last year, she'd scattered hers and Sandy's ashes onto the pile—Sandy's had been part of the legacy from her friend's cardboard box. Now, as she stood watching the ashes flutter downward, tears threatened. Quickly she turned and went to her place on the log.

The Indians lit the wooden pyre, a war whoop went up and the crowd clapped and yelled, "To victory!" Then the counselors passed out bags of marshmallows along with roasting sticks and in no time the sizzle of melting sugar blended in with the smells of night-blooming flowers and pine trees.

"This is yummy," Esther said, licking blackened goo off the end of her stick.

"Hey, Cindy!" Val called. "There's room

43

for you guys over here!"

Dawn scooted over to make room for the girls from her cabin.

"Where's Marlee?" Cindy asked.

"Who cares?" Esther said.

Dawn searched in the crowds until she finally located her standing off alone by the pier. In the shadows she looked lost, reminding Dawn of a scrawny, dejected cat. Still, she was making no effort to join in the marshmallow roast. "Maybe we should ask her over," Dawn said, pity stirring inside of her.

"Forget it," Paige said. "She tripped me when we were coming down the trail."

Dawn stared at the one-armed girl. "Are you sure? Maybe it was an accident."

"She snatched my scarf off my head," Fran offered. "And right in front of two guys. I was so embarrassed."

"She's just mean and nasty," Val said shoving another marshmallow onto her stick. "Ignore her."

Dawn decided that Val was right. If Marlee wanted to join in, she could. It was up to her. After a while the fire had burned low and cooled. Each camper had gathered ashes for the following year and they returned to their cabins.

Wearily Dawn prepared for bed, knowing that 6:00 the next morning would arrive in no time, and with it, her first full day as a CIT. She listened to the excited buzz of the girls as she turned out the lights and crawled between her fresh smelling sheets. Her feet met resistance. She pushed harder, but the sheet didn't move. Figuring it was somehow wadded up, she shoved with all her strength. She heard the sheet rip as her feet poked it.

She lay seething in the darkness. Marlee had re-made her bed all right. But the little brat had short-sheeted her.

Six

DAWN felt as if she'd barely closed her eyes when she heard her alarm clock buzz beneath her pillow. She groaned, shut if off and stumbled out of bed. Fortunately, the buzz didn't wake up any of the campers. Hurriedly, she freshened up and dressed, then headed to meet the other CITs.

"Remind me to murder Dr. Ben," Theresa grumbled to Dawn as the two of them and the other sleepy-eyed CITs stumbled into the assembly hall.

"Morning, Dawn," Brent said with a grin. "You look pretty," he whispered in her ear.

She returned his sunny smile. "Maybe we'd better get going," she suggested. "We've got to serenade 10 cabins by 7:00."

The group trudged outside where the sun was beginning to break over the tops of stately pine trees. They came to the first cabin and began singing. As Dawn heard stirrings from inside, she realized waking up to a song was better than waking up to an alarm buzzer or to a clanging bell from the mess hall.

About 30 minutes later, all the cabins had been roused and everyone had quietly assembled beside the lake where Dr. Ben spoke words of hope and encouragement. Dawn studied the campers—some on crutches, some bald, some with partial limbs, some with sores and bandages. It seemed like everyone felt perfectly free to "come as they were," without pretense or shame about how awful they might look or feel.

She remembered her first camp session with Sandy. Their hair had finally begun to grow back after chemo. In the privacy of the woods, they'd pulled off their scarves to compare lengths, and hugged each other over the progress. Absently, Dawn fingered her hair, which now brushed her shoulders. She didn't think she'd ever wear her hair short again. It brought back too many bad memories.

She was pleased to see her cabin of girls sitting together on a log. Even Marlee had turned out, though she sat hugging her knees to her chest, ignoring the other girls.

Afterward, they all filed back for breakfast and then returned to their cabins for clean-up. Dawn had been assigned CIT inspector duty for the day. When the bell had called the campers for arts and crafts, she went through each cabin with a clipboard, checking off the items that counted toward the Clean Cabin Award. Her inspection of her own cabin revealed a spotless bathroom and neatly made bunk beds—except for Marlee's.

Angry, Dawn stared down at the jumbled bedcovers. All the others were trying to win the pizza party, but Marlee wasn't co-operating. It wasn't fair. She felt like pulling the girl out of crafts and forcing her to return and make her bed. With a sigh, she decided to do it herself this one time. But she would talk to Marlee about it later.

She yanked up the satiny pink sheet and saw that it was elaborately monogrammed and trimmed in delicate eyelet lace. "Good grief," Dawn muttered. "Who brings designer sheets to camp?" She tucked in the corners and spread a beautiful, country print comforter over the sheets. "Pretty fancy," she said aloud, admiring its beauty. Certainly nicer than anything *she'd* ever owned.

Once finished, she looked around for the usual assortment of stuffed animals that girls usually brought to camp. The other beds were teeming with plush wildlife, but there were none to perch on Marlee's bed. "They all probably ran away from her," Dawn told Mr. Ruggers before leaving.

"What do you think about this, Dawn?" Paige asked the minute she stepped inside the main hall. The tiny 10-year-old held up a clear plastic bottle that she had turned into a terrarium.

"That's great," Dawn told her, inspecting the mini-jungle that Paige had carefully planted inside. Other girls came around to show off their handiwork. Everyone except Marlee had created a terrarium to take back home.

"It was stupid," Marlee told Dawn when Dawn asked her why she hadn't made one. "Who wants to take home weeds in a bottle?"

Dawn bit her tongue to keep from saying something sharp.

Right before lunch, Tony announced, "Hey, guys, Dr. Ben says the photographer's here to take the group picture. Get your suits on and meet down by the lake. Then we can swim until the lunch bell rings."

In minutes, the girls from her cabin had cleaned up the craft tables and raced to change. She followed them to the lake where a photographer arranged all the campers into a cluster and took their picture. Boys mugged and made faces, then afterward, everyone dashed for the water.

"You ready for that diving lesson?" Brent asked as she watched her kids splashing in the cool blue-green water.

"I told you, I'm hopeless. You'll be wasting your time."

"I taught one of my boys to dive already. It's simple." Still, Dawn hesitated, not wanting to embarrass herself in front of her girls. Then Brent turned to Marlee, who was just climbing up onto the pier. "Hey, Marlee. Help me show Dawn how easy it is to dive."

Without waiting for her to answer, Brent took her hand and stood beside her on the wooden dock. Dawn saw Marlee's face turn beet red. Her few tufts of hair were plastered to her scalp and her good eye darted nervously. The other was covered with a patch. Again, Dawn thought back to her first camp session when she'd felt ugly and Sandy had helped her feel better about her looks. "I'll do it if you will," Dawn suddenly blurted out, trying to help Marlee feel less in the spotlight.

By now a small group had gathered. Other voices chided, "Yeah, Marlee...do it so that she has to."

Marlee let Brent coach her for a moment before she rose on her toes, arched her arms over her head and leapt upward. Her body made a graceful straight-arrow entry into the water. The other kids clapped when she surfaced.

"Dawn's turn!" somebody yelled. Dawn made an elaborate display of backing out of her promise. But in the end she perched on the end of the dock and listened carefully to Brent's instructions. Yet when she tried to follow his directions, her arms somehow lost their arch, her legs had a mind of their own and she entered the water with an ungainly splash. She sputtered to the surface to the sound of laughter.

"Graceful as a baby hippo," Brent said from the dock, blue eyes twinkling.

She splashed water on him just as the lunch bell clanged. The campers scrambled from the lake and raced to the hall. Dawn and Brent walked at a more leisurely pace. "You were a good sport," he drawled. "Did you mess up that bad on purpose?"

"Did you pick Marlee over the others because she was having such a miserable time and needed the attention?" she countered.

Brent smiled sheepishly. "Maybe so. But she's no amateur diver, believe me."

"I thought she looked a little too grace-ful," Dawn declared.

"She's spent a lot of time getting that good. I'd say hours and hours worth of practice."

As they entered the mess hall, Dawn noticed a table had been set near the door. Dr. Ben was dispersing medications in small white cups. Dawn saw Marlee take one of the cups and felt relieved because she no longer had to endure the round of chemicals that could make a person nauseous and sick. But because she didn't have to, she felt a little guilty too.

The afternoon passed quickly and that night, after dinner, carnival night started. Each cabin set up a booth of games for campers to try. Dawn's cabin opted for the game of tossing rings around soda bottles.

Dawn spent her time retrieving rings, righting bottles, and passing out prizes. It wasn't until the bell sounded for campers to head back to their cabins that Dawn realized how exhausted she was.

She fought to keep to her eyes open while everyone got ready for bed. Girls chattered and giggled and she ruefully remembered how she and Sandy had done the same thing, never once thinking that some poor exhausted counselor wanted to sleep.

Each night, when the lights switched off, the two of them had whispered in the dark about their day's activities. Once, Dawn had crept into Sandy's bunk and they'd hidden under the covers with a flashlight and read the love scenes from a romance novel. Now, lying in the dark, waiting for the girls to quiet down, the memory returned so vividly that Dawn had to shake her head to dislodge it.

Finally everyone except Marlee was in bed. Dawn waited until she heard the bathroom door creak open and Marlee skitter across the floor. She held her breath as she heard the gentle rustle of Marlee's bedcovers, followed by tugging and yanking and tearing. From across the room, she heard Marlee hiss, "Hey! Who messed with my sheets?"

Dawn cooed sweetly in the dark, "You'd better learn to make your bed every morning if you want to avoid accidents. Good night, Marlee," she added with a satisfied yawn, then promptly fell asleep.

Seven

DAWN was eating cereal and listening to Cindy tell about her pet dog when Marlee sidled up to the table with her breakfast tray and declared, "You short-sheeted me."

Dawn looked up, prepared to receive Marlee's wrath. "You short-sheeted *me*," Dawn countered. "Around here pranks and jokes that don't hurt anybody are a way of life."

"Yeah," Fran added. "Mostly, we all try and get Dr. Ben. Dawn got him the last two years in a row." The girls who'd been to camp before told how Dawn had been the ringleader of the pranks in the past.

Marlee listened and even though she tried to act like she didn't care, Dawn saw a smile lurk at the corners of her mouth. "Why don't you sit down and have breakfast with us?" Dawn asked, casually pulling out a chair from the table.

Marlee hesitated for a second, but ended up sitting with them. *Hmm,* Dawn thought to herself. *Maybe we can soften up Marlee after all.*

"What are you going to do to him this year?" Paige asked eagerly, returning Dawn to the discussion about camp pranks.

"I'm a CIT. I'm afraid I can't do anything this year, so I guess I'll have to leave it up to you."

"Not us," Cindy said between mouthfuls of cereal. "Maybe some of the guys'll come up with an idea."

"But it's a tradition," Dawn insisted.

"Won't he get mad?" Marlee asked.

"Are you kidding?" Paige asked. "He expects it. I think we'd be letting him down if we didn't do something."

"Gee, I don't know," Val said with a shake of her head. "He'll be on the lookout so it'll really be hard to get something past him."

"Well, whatever you guys think," Dawn said, sensing the girls' hesitancy. "We can always let some of the others think one up this year."

Just then the bell clanged announcing

the end of breakfast. Fran stood, saying, "Come on, you all. Cabin clean-up. I *want* that pizza party." One by one, they started for the tray return window while Marlee sat toying with her bowl of soggy corn flakes.

Dawn held her breath, willing the others to turn around and notice. It was Val who did. "Aren't you coming, Marlee?"

Marlee started. "I—I guess so." She got up so quickly that Dawn had to catch her chair to keep it from falling over.

"Shelly's doing the inspections today," Dawn announced giving Marlee a sly wink, "so I won't be able to help you out any like I did yesterday."

"Don't worry," Esther called. "That place will be so neat, she'll be able to eat off the floors!"

Dawn watched them leave, in a cluster, like a small flock of geese. Marlee hesitated slightly, then tagged doggedly after them.

That afternoon during the rap session, Dawn and Gail led their group in a discussion about their feelings about having cancer. Dawn listened as campers shared, but she kept watching Marlee. The girl sat on her hands, her long legs wrapped around the legs of the chair, staring at the floor. Her shoulders were hunched, her back slumped. Dawn tried to pull her into the discussion, asking, "How about you, Marlee? What's your story?"

Marlee looked up and her expression reminded Dawn of a deer caught suddenly by headlights. She glanced quickly from one person to another. All at once, she announced, "This is boring. I'm out of here." She jumped up and headed out the door.

"Wait. Don't leave," Gail called and looked to Dawn. Her expression said, *Go after her.*

Dawn darted out, only to see Marlee vanishing down one of the camp trails. "Marlee!" The girl kept going and Dawn had to run to catch up. She drew alongside and grabbed her arm. "Hey, wait up."

"Leave me alone!" Marlee shouted. "I hate this place and I hate having cancer!"

She tried to shake Dawn off, but she wouldn't let go. "Do you think any of us had a choice?" Dawn asked. "No one asked me when I was 13 if I wanted to get leukemia. No one consulted me about chemo and spinal taps and blood work."

"But you're well now."

"Am I? So far my transplant's been a

success, but there are no guarantees. Come back to the group with me. Listening to the others helps you feel less alone. Who knows? Maybe it'll help make you feel better about yourself."

"I hate being defective," Marlee said bitterly. "And hanging around this place isn't going make me feel any better, no matter how much fun I try and have."

"Defective? What do you mean by that?"

"Flawed, imperfect, not right."

"So who's perfect?"

"Certainly not me," Marlee said, shaking Dawn's hand loose and running off toward the cabin.

Dawn stood in the middle of the sunlit trail and watched her disappear. She felt torn with uncertainty over helping Marlee and writing her off as hopeless. Yet she couldn't forget the look that had been on Marlee's face as she called herself defective. It was as if she felt that getting cancer had been her fault.

* * * * *

Marlee's reaction stayed in Dawn's thoughts the rest of the day. While everyone prepared for Monster Movie Night, she wandered down to the lake, sat on the end of the pier and stared out at the setting sun. "You look like you could use a friend," Brent drawled as he came up behind her.

"Hi."

He sat beside her. "I missed seeing you at dinner."

"I wasn't hungry."

"Why don't you tell me what's wrong."

"It's Marlee." From the far side of the lake, a whippoorwill called for its mate. Dawn told him about the short-sheeting episodes. "I thought she'd be really angry, but she wasn't. In fact, she ate breakfast with us." Next she told about the rap session and what Marlee had said about being defective. "And then she stayed in her bed all afternoon. I wish I knew how to get through to her."

"Why do you want to?" Brent asked.

"Because that's why I'm here—to help kids with cancer." There was more to it, but Dawn wasn't sure she could tell Brent because it involved Sandy. When Sandy had realized how shy Mike had been about his missing leg, she'd made a joke about him having more hair than she did. It had put him at ease and started their friendship. Dawn had never forgotten about her friend's sensitivity and sweetness.

Now, with Marlee, she longed for some of Sandy's compassion and instinct for saying the right thing. She glanced toward Brent. "I don't understand why Marlee's the way she is—and I want to."

"Well, maybe it would help if she fixed herself up a little."

"What do you mean?"

"She could make a little effort, you know, some make-up, covering her head—stuff like that."

"But that's the point of this place. No one has to get fixed up."

"I'll bet that Marlee never pulls herself together."

"Maybe she doesn't know how."

"I thought most girls knew how to do that stuff from birth. Sandy was always primping and Jennifer's only eight and she's already the same."

There was just enough light for her to see his eyes twinkle. She punched him playfully. "Oh, come on. Sandy and I weren't that way."

"You mean you're just naturally pretty?"

Dawn felt a fluttery sensation. "Sandy was the pretty one," she said. "I sometimes wonder just how pretty she would have been if she'd gotten to grow up."

61

"We'll never know, will we?" Brent answered. He picked up a pebble and tossed it out into the water. Dawn heard it plop and saw rings move in ever-widening circles across the surface of the tranquil lake. He shifted beside her on the dock and turned so that he was facing her. The closeness of him made her heart beat faster. He said, "I'm glad I met you, Dawn. You help me feel connected to my sister. I like the feeling. It makes me less lonely."

"You help me feel connected to her too. I guess that's the way it is with people who live with cancer. It joins you together like nothing else."

"Are you saying that if it weren't for Sandy you wouldn't even be talking to me?"

She heard the teasing tone in his voice and was grateful his mood had grown lighter, less somber. "You're the one doing all the talking," she kidded.

"Just for that, you'll have to go to the Fifties dance with me tomorrow night."

"Are you asking me or telling me?"

"Begging you."

She felt a tingly warmth spread through her. "Well, since you put it that way—it's a date." She heard the sound of her own heart thudding and hoped he couldn't hear it. She told him, "Maybe we'd better get back to the main hall. I'll bet Dr. Ben's about to start the movie."

He draped his arm around her shoulder. "We've got plenty of time. You can't watch a horror movie until it's pitch black out."

They sat on the dock watching the stars come out and the fireflies flicker and listened to bullfrogs and crickets serenade the night. She nestled against him, feeling contented. Sandy's life had made it possible for the two of them to meet. Like a connect-the-dot puzzle in a child's coloring book, cancer had joined all of them.

Which meant that she was connected to Marlee Hodges too.

Eight

WHILE the campers swam the next afternoon, the staff turned the assembly hall into a soda shop from the 1950s. Dawn couldn't believe how much work was involved. But once everything was ready, she had to admit that the effort had been worthwhile.

One side looked like a drugstore soda counter. Dr. Ben and some of the kitchen staff would serve sodas, ice cream and snacks there throughout the evening. A jukebox filled with records from the fifties had been delivered and it faced a dance floor. Pink plastic table cloths covered the tables, and cardboard cut-outs of guitars and musical notes hung on the walls.

She gave a quick, satisfied look at their work and ran back to the cabin. Before camp, a letter had been sent to the campers telling them what to bring. Dawn was pleased to see that all of them had dragged along something for Fifties Night. "What do you think of my wig?" Esther asked, turning to show off a long blond ponytail. "Don't I look awesome?"

"They didn't talk like that in the fifties, silly," Fran said laughing. "They would have said you look *cool*," she added.

By the time Dawn showered, dressed in her mother's old poodle skirt, bobby socks and saddle shoes and arrived at the hall, the place was jumping. An old song by Elvis was playing on the jukebox and in the center of the floor, Brent was doing a terrific impression of the king of rock and roll. He'd blackened his hair, slicked it back on the sides and was wearing a jacket that glittered in the light. Every time he gyrated, the girls would squeal and shriek.

Dawn searched the room until she spied Marlee sitting off by herself. She approached and asked above the noise, "Can I join you?" Startled, Marlee nodded. "So what do you think?" Dawn asked.

Marlee was watching Brent with a look in her eyes that almost looked like longing. "He makes a good Elvis."

"There're some cute guys here, don't you

think?" Dawn said, gesturing toward groups of boys near the jukebox.

"They're all geeks."

"They're not *that* bad."

"I think they are."

Just then, Brent came dancing toward them, a cluster of young girls squealing after him. He stopped in front of Dawn and Marlee and continued his number. Dawn laughed, but Marlee turned bright red. Brent held out his hand to her, but Marlee shrank back and refused it.

"Dance with Elvis, Marlee!" someone shouted.

Marlee shook her head furiously. Brent held out his arms again, but she sat on her hands. To help Marlee out of her embarrassment, Dawn jumped up and grabbed Brent's hand. They bopped and twirled while the crowd clapped. As the song wound down, Brent hung onto to Dawn, waved to his admirers and dashed out the door, pulling her along behind him.

"Elvis! Come back!" girls' voices shouted.

"In a minute!" he told them.

Together Brent and Dawn ran through the woods laughing. They stopped finally, breathless and still giggling. Dawn said, "You can't run out on your fans like that,

Elvis."

Brent leaned against a tree and took in great gulps of air. "It's not easy being a legend, you know. I think I dislocated my hips."

"Wasn't it worth it? Look at all the girls falling at your feet." She fluttered her eyelashes. "Look at all the hearts you won."

The moon overhead flickered through the trees and she saw his eyes sparkle. "I prefer the hearts of big girls," he said.

Dawn's mouth went dry and her head felt suddenly light. "Marlee couldn't take her eyes off you. I think she has a crush on you. I'm glad you asked her to dance with you."

"I think I embarrassed her."

"Probably, but it's a really good kind of embarrassment."

"There are good and bad kinds?"

"Sure. When you trip in the lunchroom and drop a tray of food and everybody stares at you—that's a bad kind. But when Elvis picks *you* to dance from all the rest...." She let the sentence trail off.

He accepted her good-natured kidding. "Why's it so important to you that Marlee have a good time?"

"Maybe because she's so dead set against

having one."

"Dawn Rochelle to the rescue? Is that your life mission?"

Dawn poked him. "Never! By the way, your hair color's running, mister rock star."

Brent tried to wipe off his forehead, which in the moon's light looked streaked with black rivulets. All he did was smear them around.

"Let me," Dawn insisted between fits of giggles. She found a tissue wadded up in the pocket of her skirt and blotted his forehead. She was so close she could feel his breath on her cheek. He smelled of peppermint.

Brent's hand caught hers and stopped its motion. His skin felt warm. Her gaze drifted into his and her heart hammered. He tilted her chin upward and lowered his mouth. He was inches away from kissing her when she heard shuffling in the bushes. Her back stiffened. "What's that noise?"

Brent paused, but didn't take his gaze from her face. "I don't hear anything."

"There it is again." She listened as leaves rustled and voices murmured.

Suddenly, from out of the darkness she heard a symphony of high, small voices sing out, "Dawn and Brent are sitting in a tree k-i-s-s-i-n-g!"

"Val, Fran, Esther—is that you?" Dawn called, her face hot with self-conscious color.

"Friends of yours?" Brent teased.

"We followed you, Elvis." Paige's voice answered from the bushes.

"I think we should catch them all and throw them in the lake," Brent announced while nudging Dawn and pointing in the direction of the voices.

"That'll teach them to spy," she added and ran toward the clump of bushes.

Five girls shrieked and scattered, darting between trees and yelling, "You can't catch me!"

They chased one another like frisky puppies in the moonlight while the woods rang with their high-pitched laughter. Dawn understood their jubilation. She was reminded of the night she and Sandy had stolen Dr. Ben's underwear and had dashed through the woods trying to hold back their laughter. She'd felt giddy and bubbly because they'd succeeded. But it had been more than the joke that had made them feel good. They'd been together and that had made the moment even more special and memorable.

Don't think about it, she told herself. *Just think about tonight and these girls.* She tried. But, like the moonlight slipping through the leafy trees, the image of Sandy clutched at her memory and refused to go.

* * * * *

By the time Dawn and Brent had helped clean up after the dance and Dawn had arrived back at her cabin, it was almost lights-out. In the cabin, the girls were sprawled across two bottom bunks, nibbling on candy bars and poring through a heap of eyeshadows, lipsticks and blushers.

"Where's Gail?" Dawn asked, coming over to them.

"Oh, some kid in cabin five got really sick and so she went to help out," Fran said matter-of-factly. "His chemo is all messed up and they may have to send him home."

Dawn felt sorry for the boy, but she didn't want her girls to dwell on it. Cheerfully, she asked, "So what are you doing?"

"Trying on make-up," Paige told her. Dawn joined them on one of the bunks.

"Are you mad at us for interrupting you and Brent?" Paige asked shyly.

Dawn ruffled her hair. "Of course not."

"So what's it like being kissed?" Val asked.

Dawn felt warm all over. "Isn't it time for lights out?"

"Nope."

Dawn glanced at the eager faces. At the very back of one bunk, with her backbone pressed to the wall, sat Marlee. She reminded Dawn of someone hanging around the edge of a campfire—hungry and eager to get warm, but afraid to come too close.

Cindy flopped over on her tummy and tucked a pillow under her chest. "I've been kissed before," she announced.

"By who? Your dog?" Esther asked.

The others laughed and Cindy stuck out her tongue. "It was at a party with kids from school. We were playing a kissing game and I ended up with Mark Bresford and all the other girls were jealous because they all had a crush on him and I got him."

"So what was it like?" Fran asked, eagerly. She'd untied her scarf from her bald head and it had slid unnoticed to the bed.

Cindy wrinkled her nose. "Wet."

"I told you it was her dog." Esther said.

Val let out an exasperated squeak and rolled over on the bed. "Some romantic story that is, Cindy."

"You've got a better one?"

"Aw, who wants to kiss a girl who's bald and barfing?"

"It can happen," Dawn heard herself say.

All eyes turned toward her. "Someone kissed you when you looked all wasted from chemo?" Fran asked, wide-eyed. "Tell us. Tell us all about it."

Nine

NATURALLY, Dawn hadn't meant to tell them about it. But hearing how a few of them longed to be kissed and how unattractive they felt about themselves, she just couldn't help herself. "I-it was at camp."

"Oh, so he was a chemo geek too," Esther said with an understanding bob of her head.

"That's not a very nice thing to say," Paige scolded. "Dawn's pretty. She's probably been kissed hundreds of times."

"Half a hundred," Dawn joked, making the others laugh. *Actually only once*, she thought. It would have been twice if they hadn't interrupted Brent earlier.

"All right, so some guy kissed you at camp. But what about a *normal* guy—one who doesn't have cancer."

73

"Yeah—do you have a boyfriend?" Paige asked, scooting closer on the bed. The empty sleeve of her nightshirt swayed with the movement.

Instantly, Dawn thought about Jake Macka. "Well, I liked a guy once from school."

"Who was he? What did he look like?" Cindy wanted to know.

"His name was Jake and he had black hair and gorgeous brown eyes. He sent me a card when I was in the hospital the first time—at least, I always suspected it was him. It wasn't signed."

"What happened to him?"

"He moved away."

"But didn't anything *happen* between you?" Cindy sounded disappointed.

"We didn't kiss if that's what you mean, but I've never felt about anyone else the way I felt about him."

"Not even Brent?" Val asked.

Dawn thought about it. Brent had a way of making her feel gooey inside. And she certainly had wanted him to kiss her, but it *was* different than it had been with Jake. She wished she could put it into words, but she couldn't. "I've only known Brent a few days," she said. "And besides, it's

74

summer and everyone knows about summer romances."

"I don't," Paige said, wide-eyed.

They all burst out laughing. "Everybody falls in love in the summer," explained Dawn. "But when school starts—well, summer love fades like a summer tan."

"Oh."

Paige sounded so disappointed that they all laughed again. Dawn fingered the pile of make-up in the middle of the bed. "So, what're you going to do with all this stuff?" she asked.

"We thought we'd practice different looks," Cindy said, rummaging through the little pots of eye color.

"My dad says I can't wear make-up until I'm 13," Paige declared. "But since I've only got one arm, I figure I'd better start practicing putting it on now."

Dawn chose a tube of colored mascara and held it up. "Um, Marlee, why don't you try navy blue eye shadow?"

At the sound of her name, Marlee looked startled. She'd been so quiet that the others had probably forgotten she was still with them. "Uh, no...I don't want to."

"Don't be a party pooper," Esther said, as she stared into a hand mirror and smeared frosted green shadow across her eyelid.

"I told you I don't want to."

"Well, okay. We just thought you might like to join in."

"Well, I don't." Marlee scrambled off the bed, knocking Esther's arm and causing her to smear shadow onto her forehead.

"Hey! Now look at the mess you made."

Marlee hustled outside and while the girls grumbled, Dawn went out after her. She hoped Marlee wouldn't take off running as she had before. It was too dark to chase her through the woods. She was relieved to find Marlee at the bottom of the porch steps, where she was standing barefoot on the damp grass.

"They just didn't want you to feel left out," Dawn said, defending the group.

"I don't wear make-up," Marlee said flatly.

For an instant, Dawn felt anger boil inside her. She wanted to shake the girl. People had bent over backwards to reach out to Marlee, but she wouldn't even try to meet them halfway. "Don't stay outside too long. It's past curfew," Dawn told her icily.

She started back up the steps when she

heard Marlee say in a small voice, "It's because of my eye."

Dawn stopped. "Your eye?"

"The fake one."

Dawn came slowly back down the steps to stand next to Marlee. "What about it?"

"After the doctors cut out my eye and gave me this glass one, I tried to put make-up on. The tear duct's still there and it kept watering and watering. Pretty soon, eye shadow and mascara were running down my face until I looked like a freak. There's no such thing as a really water-proof mascara you know, even though the ads in the magazines say that there is."

In the moonlight, Dawn saw that tears were trickling down Marlee's cheek.

"I was a real mess. When I finally got cleaned up, my lashes were stuck shut to-gether. After all the moisture, the socket suddenly got dried out. So now I don't wear any make-up. Ever."

Dawn's chest felt as if a weight were pressing against it. "There must be women who have glass eyes and know how to manage make-up. I've read about actresses in Hollywood who—"

"Why should I bother?" Marlee's voice trembled. "I'm ugly and no amount of make-up's going to change that."

"You're not ugly, Marlee. You just *feel* ugly," Dawn told her, recalling some of the things she'd been told by hospital psychologists. "The way you feel doesn't mean that's the way you really *are*."

"I wasn't pretty before I got cancer," she answered bitterly. "And now...well, mirrors don't lie."

Dawn searched for something encouraging to say. "You're a great diver. Brent told me so."

"He did?"

"He said he could tell that you practiced a lot."

"I love to swim and dive. I live with my grandmother and she has an indoor pool and I practice all the time. That's something else I had to learn to do all over again after my eye surgery—diving."

"You did?"

"When you only have one eye, it affects your depth perception. I couldn't measure the distance to the water by looking at it. The first time I tried to dive after the operation, I almost killed myself."

"But you kept trying, because I saw you dive the other day and you were really good."

"I worked harder than I've ever worked on anything before," Marlee said softly.

"Well, you can do the same thing with make-up and mascara. You just have to keep practicing."

Marlee hung her head and drew a pattern in the grass with her big toe. "You think that's all there is to it?"

"You won't know if you don't try."

"I don't know..."

"We could go try right now. I could help and so would the others."

"They hate me."

"Wrong. They may hate the way you act, but they don't really know *you*."

"I'm pretty forgettable."

Dawn put her arm around Marlee's thin shoulders. "You're a lot of things, Marlee Hodges, but forgettable isn't one of them."

Marlee tipped her head back and studied Dawn through one partially closed eyelid. The other lid drooped noticeably over her glass eye. "You're not just saying that to butter me up, are you?"

Dawn laughed over Marlee's sudden turn to dry humor. "I've only got two more days to make sure you have a good time," she said, leading her up the porch steps toward the cabin where the others could be heard joking over newly made-up faces. "You can't let my very first job as a CIT be a failure."

The door banged shut behind them as they walked out of the night and into the light.

Ten

DAWN considered that night a turning point for Marlee. She had gone back inside the cabin and let Dawn apply the cosmetics, including eyeliner and mascara. Marlee tried on one of Fran's wigs and one of Cindy's outfits. And in the end, the results had been dramatic. "You look super," Dawn told her. And she meant it.

But the biggest benefit was that the evening had built a bridge between Marlee and the other girls. Not that Marlee became Little Miss Sunshine, but she did lighten up. She was less critical of people and camp activities. She made up her bed each morning and actually participated in arts and crafts. The others invited her to sit with them during meals and included her in their discussions after lights out.

Dawn felt pleased with the way things

were going and faced Friday, the last full day of camp and the Junior Olympics, with mixed emotions. On the one hand, she was anxious to get home and get on with her summer. On the other, it was going to be hard to say good-bye to everyone.

Area reporters and a TV crew showed up to cover the games. Overall, Dawn's girls did well in the individual events. They won the egg toss—Paige turned out to be an ace egg heaver with her one arm—and placed third in the mushy oatmeal pass. Yet the big finale—the Great American Tug of War, as Dr. Ben called it—turned out to be the highlight of the games.

In the center of the playing field, the staff created an enormous mudhole, a large sticky pit of goo that resembled a vat of chocolate in the hot afternoon sunlight. The campers formed two teams, each with their quota of counselors, medical helpers, CITs and campers. Soon each team was lined up on the wet grass with a thick rope stretched between them. A bright red rag, tied to the center of the rope, dangled over the pit of dark, oozing mud. The first team to bring the rag to their side of the mud hole would win.

"Of course, if anyone just *happens* to fall

into the mud, then it's too bad," Dr. Ben told the audience as he grabbed hold of the thick rope at the front of the line.

Dawn stood midway in the line behind Dr. Ben, in front of Val and behind Marlee as the rope went taut. On the other team, Brent shouted instructions to his teammates. Instantly, she felt herself sliding forward. She gritted her teeth and pulled, using all her strength.

Someone shouted, "Dig in!" Dawn stomped her feet hard and felt her sneakers sink slightly into the wet ground. Slowly she stopped her forward slide.

"Heave!" someone else yelled. She groaned and jerked harder. She saw Marlee's shoulders hunch in front of her. "Whose dumb idea was this?" Marlee managed to ask through clenched teeth.

"Just keep pulling!" Dawn commanded. "Or we'll be eating mud pies!"

From the front, she heard Dr. Ben holler, "We're gaining! We're gaining!" Immediately, her sneakers began to slide forward. Dr. Ben yelped, "We're giving! We're giving!"

For some reason, his words struck Dawn as funny and she began to giggle. Her laughter was contagious. Val started snickering, then Marlee, then the kid behind her, and so on, until everyone was laughing. As the laughter swelled, everyone's strength gave out and the whole group started sliding faster and faster toward the mud hole.

Dr. Ben shouted, "Stop that noise! This is treason! Treason!" But, like dominoes, the line began to falter and finally to topple. And because he was first in the line, Dr. Ben tumbled spread-eagle into the gooey mud.

Dawn lay flat on the ground holding her sides, weak with laughter. Marlee lay beside her and members from the other team wandered over. "You didn't put up much of a fight," Brent said, plopping down next to them.

Cameras clicked and reporters called out joking remarks as Dr. Ben walked past, his front covered with brown gook. Dawn took one look and started laughing again.

"You think this is funny?" Dr. Ben asked, pretending to be angry. He smeared a dollop of mud on her nose. She only laughed harder.

"Don't forget this one," Brent shouted, scooping a handful of mud from the doctor's arm and splattering it on Marlee.

"Hey!" Marlee squealed, grabbing a handful of her own and smearing it on him.

In seconds, a mud-slinging war had erupted. Campers, counselors, even a few reporters began hurling globs of mud at one another. Kids rolled on the grass and slathered one another with brown wet dirt. Girls ran shrieking as boys threatened to toss them into the sea of mud. Cameras clicked and video cameras hummed, recording the entire mess.

With her sides aching from laughter, Dawn stepped back and watched the fun. A memory from her first Junior Olympics slipped into her mind. She saw Sandy smiling triumphantly as her team won the water balloon toss. *If only you were here,* Dawn thought to herself. *If only we could be doing this together.*

Brent came up beside her. "You giving up?" he asked.

His question jerked her back into the present. "Never," she said, with a huskiness in her voice that made him peer at her more closely.

"You okay?"

"Fine," she told him. "Never been better."

"You looked sort of lonesome standing off by yourself."

She poked him in the ribs. "And *you* look like a pig who's lost his pen."

"A pig!" he cried.

With a laugh, she shoved him away and darted off. He chased her and they zigzagged under the hot sun until Dawn was completely exhausted. Too exhausted to think about Sandy for the rest of the day.

* * * * *

That night in the main hall, Dr. Ben gave out awards and ribbons for all the week's activities. "Now, here's the one I know you've all been waiting for," the doctor said. "The coveted Clean Cabin Award."

Excited whispers rustled through the crowd. Val leaned over to Dawn and asked, "Do you know who got it?"

"Nope. It's a big surprise, even for the CITs."

Dr. Ben continued. "I tallied up all the points from each of the CITs' reports and I'm pleased to announce the grand prize winner. There are four large pizzas waiting in the kitchen for the winners to take back to their cabin while the rest of us make do on punch and cookies."

The crowd booed. Dr. Ben held up his

hand. "Those are the rules, folks. The winners get to pig out. When I call out the winner, send one representative to claim your prize. The pizza man's waiting in the kitchen." He turned toward his helper. "May I have the envelope, please."

She handed him a white envelope. Then he ripped it open and pulled out a piece of paper. After a dramatic pause he read, "The winner is: Cabin Three."

Dawn and her kids shrieked and hugged one another. Dawn shoved Marlee forward and whispered, "Go collect and we'll meet you by the kitchen door."

Marlee hurried forward, while boys from other cabins made outrageous promises to her if only she'd share the pizza with them. At the mike, Dr. Ben held out his hand and Marlee shook it. All at once, there was a thunking sound, as something hard and small hit the wooden floor.

Marlee grabbed the side of her face and squealed, "My eye! Dr. Ben, my glass eye fell out!"

Gasping, Dr. Ben dropped to the floor on all fours and started crawling around. Suddenly, Marlee's hands opened and fistfuls of small glass marbles cascaded over the floor, bouncing and thunking in every direction.

Scrambling, Dr. Ben struggled frantically to retrieve them. "Wait, I've got it! No, that's not it! Here it is!"

Dawn was one of the first to catch on to Marlee's gag, so she started laughing and pointing.

Dr. Ben stopped crawling and looked up at Marlee, whose face broke into an impish grin. "Got you, Dr. Ben," she said.

He groaned and shook his head, smiled sheepishly, and sat down on the floor amid a hundred shiny glass marbles.

Pandemonium broke out as all the campers and counselors caught onto the joke. They whistled, clapped and shouted, "Marlee! Marlee!" A brilliant smile lit up Marlee's face.

Like radar, Dr. Ben's gaze locked onto Dawn's, and she saw him wink. She nodded in understanding, and, like an accomplice, winked back at him. Of course, he'd known that Marlee's eye could never have fallen out. But he'd gone along with the prank and given the girl a moment she'd always remember. A lump the size of a handful of marbles rose in Dawn's throat. And at that second she loved dear Dr. Ben with all her heart.

Eleven

IT rained the next day. As the girls in Dawn's cabin packed up to go home, the atmosphere was gloomy. "This is the worst part," Cindy groused as she shoved clothes into her duffel bag. "I just hate saying good-bye."

"We can write each other," Paige offered eagerly.

"Oh, we'll write each other for a while," Esther said. "But then we'll get busy with school and stuff and we'll forget."

"Well, we'll see each other next summer," Val declared.

Dawn listened to them make plans as she folded up her bed linen. She kept thinking back to when she told Sandy goodbye for the last time. They'd promised to write and meet again the following summer. After Sandy had died, she'd tied up all of Sandy's wonderful letters and put them in the cardboard box.

You've got to stop this remembering, Dawn told herself sternly. It wasn't helping her mood any. "I've got an umbrella," she announced to the girls as they packed. "When you're ready to take your gear to the main hall, let me know."

Later, she walked them in groups of two while holding the umbrella as the rain fell steady and fine, turning the trails to slippery paths. Cars and vans clustered in the parking lot near the hall where kids and parents greeted one another. She hugged her girls goodbye, then went back to the cabin to collect her own gear.

Inside the cabin, gloom had settled. The smell of hair spray, perfume, and baby powder lingered in the air, but the building looked sad without all the hustle and bustle of the girls.

"Anybody here?" Brent's voice called through the screen door.

"Just me," Dawn said, grabbing up her bags and crossing to the door.

He stood on the porch in a yellow rain slicker, his hair wet with rain. She was glad to see him. Standing alone in the damp, dreary cabin remembering that other summer so vividly had become almost too much for her to bear.

"Let me help," he said, taking the bags.

"I'm not in a big hurry," she confessed. "I told Rob to be here by 1:00 because I figured everyone would be gone by then. Maybe we can just wait here on the porch until the crowd thins out."

He set her bag down, removed his slicker and draped it over the railing next to her. "You okay?" he asked.

She stared out at the drizzling rain. "Sure. It's just that leaving is sort of sad."

"You can come back next year and see everybody."

"That's what the girls said."

"But you don't want to come back?" His expression looked quizzical. "Didn't you have a good time?"

"I had a great time. It's just that..." She searched for words to express her feelings. "I don't know how to say it."

His blue eyes looked knowingly into hers. "It's just that maybe someone will die before next summer rolls around."

"How'd you know?"

"I felt the same way when Sandy went off to Mexico. I knew there was a chance I'd never see her alive again. It turned out

I never did."

She shivered slightly and Brent put his arm around her and pulled her to his side. He felt solid and warm against her skin. "You've still got another week here, don't you?"

"Sure do. The sibling campers check in tomorrow."

"What'll you do until then?"

"I'm going into town with some of the staff. We've got to hit a laundromat first. After the mud war, my clothes look pretty grim." He wrinkled his nose. "They don't smell so sweet either. Then we'll take in a movie and come back here and get ready to face a new group tomorrow."

She realized suddenly that she'd miss seeing Brent every day too. "Did you enjoy doing this camp?"

"I really did. It took a day or so for me to adjust to the ones with cut-off limbs and bald heads and all. But deep down they're just regular kids who got handed a bum rap from life." He gazed down at her. "You glad you did it?"

"I sure am. They're a pretty terrific bunch of kids."

"Even Marlee?"

Dawn laughed. "I think she thawed out

and had fun toward the end—even though she tried hard not to."

"You could thaw anyone out, Dawn."

His beautiful blue eyes stared into hers. She felt her knees go weak. "I, uh, had my doubts about Marlee for a while," she added. "If she comes back next year, it'll be proof that she had a good time."

He turned her to face him. "Can I write you?"

"Uh, sure."

He smoothed her hair and said, "You've got pretty hair."

"Thank you."

"You know what?"

"What?"

"I never got that kiss."

"We kept getting interrupted."

He glanced about. The steady beat of the rain sounded muffled as it struck trees and foliage. "No one's here now to interrupt."

"That's true," Dawn whispered.

His arms slipped around her waist and her arms entwined around his neck. Dawn felt herself rise onto her toes and her chin lift. They stood on the porch wrapped in the sound of summer rain, his kiss resting like soft petals on her lips.

* * * * *

When she was certain that the campers had gone, Dawn walked alone to the hall with her things. Brent had left when Dr. Ben had shouted to him that the van was heading for town. "I'll write," he promised her, then bounded down the steps.

The rain had stopped, but the afternoon still looked gloomy as she made her way along the trail. She entered the hall and heard the sounds of pots and pans, signaling that the kitchen help was organizing for the next group of campers. In a far corner, Dawn saw a figure hunched over a leather suitcase. Surprised, she asked, "Marlee? Are you still here?"

The 13-year-old straightened. "Yeah."

Dawn approached, remembering that Marlee had no parents to pick her up. "How are you getting home? Is your grandmother coming for you?"

"Grams doesn't drive. She's got a heart problem."

"Gee, I'm sorry."

"Don't apologize. It's not your fault," Marlee said a bit sarcastically. "I've been living with her since my parents died when I was five. She's always been sick."

"Well, do you have any brothers or sisters?" Dawn asked awkwardly.

"Just me and Grams." Marlee heaved a deep sigh.

"Why don't I wait with you? My brother's not supposed to be here to pick me up for another half-hour."

"I'm not a baby, you know. I can wait by myself."

Dawn gritted her teeth. The old Marlee was back. Why did she make it so hard to be nice to her? "Can I sit with you anyway?" Dawn asked.

"It's a free country."

Dawn plopped onto the bench, determined not to let Marlee get under her skin. She asked, "So did you have a good time at camp?"

"It was all right."

"Just all right? You'll go down in camp history for getting Dr. Ben the way you did."

A small smile softened Marlee's mouth. "I got him good didn't I?" Suddenly, the girl swung around to straddle the bench and face Dawn. "I heard the other girls say they'd write to each other. Will you write me?"

Marlee's about-face surprised Dawn. One minute she acted hateful, the next, friendly. Would she ever figure her out?

"We both live in Columbus, why don't you call me sometime?" Dawn suggested.

"You won't mind?"

"Of course not," Dawn said. "Hey, here comes a car. I'll bet it's your ride." Dawn jumped up and peered through the rain-spotted window and watched a long black limousine crunch over the wet gravel.

"Yeah," Marlee said listlessly. "It's Grams' chauffeur."

"That's your grandmother's car?"

Marlee dragged her suitcase outside without answering. Dawn followed. The driver's door opened and a man in a uniform got out. "Miss Marlee," he said with a smile. "I'm sorry I'm running late."

"How's Grams?"

"She was feeling rather poorly today. She sent me to fetch you. Said to tell you she's very sorry she couldn't come along."

Marlee's expression had become a dull mask. "It's no big deal."

The chauffeur placed the luggage in the trunk and opened the car door to the back seat. Dawn had a glimpse of a rich gray velour interior as Marlee crawled inside. "Call me," Dawn said hastily.

"Okay," Marlee answered.

The chauffeur returned behind the

wheel, put the car into gear and swung it around toward the gravel road. Dawn watched as the sleek black car inched along. Its gleaming metal and smoky dark windows reflected the rays of a weak sun that had emerged from behind clouds. She watched until it disappeared through the forest of green, leafy trees.

Twelve

"TELL me everything that happened and don't scrimp on the details," Dawn's friend, Rhonda Watson, said eagerly the day after Dawn had returned from camp.

Dawn shut her bedroom door and let Rhonda haul her across the room and push her onto the bed. "You must be starved for news," Dawn kidded. "I thought *you'd* be the one with stories to tell."

Rhonda rolled her eyes and dragged Dawn's half-unpacked bag onto the floor. Clothes tumbled onto the carpet. "You don't know what it's been like around here. Boring wouldn't *begin* to describe it."

"First, what about the job? Is it still open?" Dawn was anxious to hear if she'd still be working at the ice cream parlor. Now that camp was behind her, she couldn't wait to start her first real job.

"Of course, it's open. Three afternoons a week and all day Saturdays."

Relieved, Dawn said, "Good. I'm saving every penny I make for school clothes. I really want to look like dynamite when we start in September."

"Now tell me about camp before I explode!" Rhonda insisted.

She did look ready to pop, so Dawn began unfolding her tale of camp life. She told her about Marlee. Rhonda wrinkled her nose. "Sounds like she's related to my brother. He's taken being a brat to new heights, you know."

"Marlee wasn't always a brat. Sometimes she tried hard, like the time the girls decided to experiment with make-up. We all had a good time that night." Dawn picked Mr. Ruggers off the floor and wrapped her arms around his fuzzy body.

"And she really did have things stacked against her," she added. "Can you imagine growing up without parents? Plus losing an eye?"

"But you said she was rich. That part must be fun."

"I *think* she's rich. I'm not sure. But riding in a limo and having designer sheets can't make up for all the rest."

Rhonda offered a sympathetic shrug of her shoulders. "Was Marlee the only interesting person at camp?" she asked.

"There might have been one other."

Rhonda stared at her for a second. Dawn tried to keep a straight face, but the corners of her mouth kept turning up. Rhonda's eyes grew wide. She blurted, "Dawn Rochelle! You rat! You met a guy, didn't you?"

Dawn burst out laughing as Rhonda pounced on her. "Tell me everything," Rhonda demanded.

"Okay. Get off me."

Rhonda obliged and after Dawn caught her breath, she told Rhonda about Brent. "Lucky you," Rhonda sighed. "He sounds totally awesome. Are you going to see him again?"

Dawn thought about her answer, because actually she had very mixed feelings about Brent. She really liked being with him, but she also realized that her attraction for him was somehow tied up in his being Sandy's brother. He was a link to her friend, a living bridge to her memory. She couldn't explain it to Rhonda—she could scarcely understand it herself. So she told

Rhonda the things she could explain. "He's starting college in the fall."

"So what?"

"Think about it, Rhonda. I'm going to be a high school sophomore. By the time he settles into campus life and meets college girls, I'll just be a kid to him."

"Sort of like my crush on Rob, huh?"

Rhonda's mention of her attraction for Rob caused Dawn to smile kindly. "Well, Rob does talk about Katie a lot," she told her friend, trying to let her down easy.

"I know. It was always the impossible dream for me. Sort of like having a crush on a movie star." Rhonda hunkered down on the bed and gazed thoughtfully up at Dawn. "But let's not write this Brent off for you too prematurely."

"Oh Rhonda—"

"Don't 'oh, Rhonda' me." The brown-haired girl declared. "What are you going to do if he calls you? Hang up on him?"

"Of course not."

"Then who knows? There may be hope for the two of you yet."

Dawn flung Mr. Ruggers playfully at her friend. "Let's forget camp and think about the rest of the summer. I can't wait to start my job."

"We'll go in together early Saturday. That way I can give you your apron and cap and show you the ropes. It's fun, and sometimes really cute guys stop in."

Dawn flopped back on her bed in exasperation. "Is that *all* you ever think about? Meeting guys?"

"No way," Rhonda said with an indignant sniff. "I also think about Fudge Ripple, Rocky Road, French Vanilla—"

Dawn squealed and threw a pillow at her friend. Together, laughing and tickling, they tumbled to the floor like playful kittens.

* * * * *

By the middle of July, Dawn had settled into a pleasant routine. She slept late, watched a few game shows, did chores for her Mom, read novels and went to work. Brent wrote, full of news about sibling cancer camp and getting ready for college. She enjoyed getting his letters and hoped her letters to him sounded half as interesting to him.

She loved her job. The ice cream parlor was a tiny little cubby hole in the mall, just big enough for five small glass-topped tables and old-fashioned parlor chairs. She and Rhonda worked behind a counter that doubled as a freezer case filled with vats of ice cream. She learned to run a cash register and to make milkshakes, hot fudge sundaes, banana splits and the Monster Bowl—a giant concoction made up of a scoop of every flavor, swimming in toppings, whipped cream and nuts.

Mostly, people bought cones to go, but sometimes every table would be filled with customers and Dawn felt as if she were drowning in ice cream orders. Rob and Katie often dropped in and Dawn could see their happiness spilling out of their smiles.

"You never come see me on the floor," Katie grumbled good-naturedly during one visit when Rob had stepped into the washroom.

Dawn knew she was talking about the pediatric oncology floor at the hospital. "No offense," Dawn said. "But I've seen all I want to see of that place." *I almost died there*, she thought.

Katie nibbled on a nut embedded in her butter pecan cone. "Joan Clark tells me that you were a fabulous CIT. The staff and the kids really liked you."

Dawn was pleased by the compliment. "They were a pretty nice bunch. I had a good time."

"Think you'll do it again next year?"

Dawn hesitated to say yes. She was having such a wonderful time being a normal, regular, ordinary, typical 15-year-old girl that she hated to be reminded about her leukemia. Except for her clinic visits and blood work, parts of the past seemed only like a bad dream. "I'm not sure," she told Katie. "I think I'd like to try working full-time next summer."

"Too bad," Katie answered. "You're a real inspiration to some child going through it."

Dawn wanted to tell her that it was hard being an inspiration. But Rhonda interrupted just then. "Good grief," she cried. "Look! A whole busload of senior citizens is coming straight toward us."

"We better get busy," Dawn told Katie with a bright smile.

"Well, come and see me at work sometime," she called, taking Rob's hand as he came up beside her.

"I will," Dawn said, knowing deep down that she wouldn't willingly go up to the oncology floor ever again!

*   *   *   *   *

The next Friday night, Dawn was sitting in the living room watching TV with her parents when the phone rang. "I'll get it." She hurried to the kitchen phone for privacy.

"Can I speak to Dawn, please?" The girl's voice on the other end of the receiver sounded quivery and familiar.

"This is Dawn. Who's this?"

"I-it's me—Marlee Hodges."

For no reason, Dawn's heart skipped a beat. "Hi. How are you? Is everything all right?"

"No." Marlee's voice wavered.

Dawn clutched the receiver so tightly that her fingers hurt. "What's wrong?"

"I'm back in the hospital and I'm scared. Please, come see me, Dawn. Please."

Thirteen

DAWN watched the elevator doors slide open. Beyond them, lay the brightly lit corridors of the pediatric oncology floor. The walls were painted a sunny yellow and decorated with life-size drawings of cartoon characters. A nurses' station formed a hub in the center of the floor and hallways stretched in three different directions. Down one wing, infants and children under age six were treated. Down another, older children and teens roomed. And down the third was the critical care unit. Dawn remembered with a shudder the weeks she'd spent in isolation down that particular corridor.

She passed the activity room and paused at the doorway. Intense Saturday morning sunlight streamed through the wall of windows. Memories of the time she'd spent doing craft projects with Sandy swirled through her mind. Sandy had fashioned a necklace of popcorn and sprinkled it with glitter. Dawn had decorated a drawing of a teddy bear with popped kernels to make it look furry. A popcorn war had broken out, with popcorn flying everywhere. And they had laughed and laughed. Dawn could almost hear their laughter still...

With a sigh, she shoved away from the doorway. She was here to visit Marlee, not old memories. The girl had sounded so frightened on the phone the night before. Dawn passed the nurse's station. Katie wasn't on duty today and she didn't recognize any of the other faces. *Everything changes*, she reminded herself. Dawn found Marlee's room, squared her shoulders and pushed open the door.

Marlee was in bed, watching TV. The room was private, spacious and sunny. A mauve fabric sofa, chair and small table in one area made it seem more like a hotel suite than a hospital room. The metal IV stand beside Marlee's bed and hooked to her wrist was the only thing that made the room look like a hospital room.

"Good morning," Dawn said. "Are the good guys winning?"

Marlee flipped off the TV with the remote. "You came!" she said. "I'm so glad you came." Marlee was smiling, but her face looked small and pinched, pale in the bright room. Her tiny body seemed lost on the big bed.

"I told you I'd come." Dawn dragged a chair beside Marlee's bed. "Tell me what happened?"

"I started vomiting yesterday morning and couldn't stop. And I had this terrible stomach-ache." She rubbed her tummy under the bedcovers. "Grams called my doctor and he put me right into the hospital."

"Maybe it's the flu. People can catch a flu bug in the summer. Or a leftover from camp food—at least I *think* it was food." Dawn made a face as she said it.

Marlee refused to smile. "They took a bunch of X-rays last night. They wouldn't take X-rays for the flu."

Dawn chewed on her lower lip. "Has your doctor been in to see you yet?"

"No. He said he had to consult with another doctor. You know how it is."

Dawn knew how it was. In her case, specialists consulted with specialists and decisions were made and medicines were prescribed and no one ever asked her how she felt about any of it. At one time, there had been six doctors consulting about her treatments. "So is your grandmother here?"

"Not yet. She wasn't feeling good when we talked on the phone last night."

"Well, maybe she's better this morning," Dawn offered cheerfully.

Marlee plucked at the sheet. "Yeah. But all this is hard on her heart and all. I wish I hadn't gotten sick."

Marlee's feistiness had gone out of her and Dawn suddenly missed it. She rose from the chair and made a tour of the room. "I didn't know this place had such nice rooms. You should see where they stuck me. It was barely bigger than my locker at school. And I had a roommate too. Her name was Sandy. We were like sisters."

"I used to wish that I had a sister," Marlee said shyly. "Sometimes when I was growing up, I'd get so lonely." She gave a hapless shrug. "And so I thought it would be nice to have a sister. If I ever get married, I'm going to have a whole bunch of kids."

Marlee's admission surprised Dawn. She crossed the room to stand by the metal IV apparatus. "At camp you acted like you wanted to be left alone—like you didn't want to be around the other girls."

"But I *did* want to. They just really didn't like me."

Dawn wanted to remind Marlee that her rudeness had driven the other girls away, but it didn't seem like good timing. "So is that why you called me last night? Because you're lonesome?"

Marlee didn't answer right away. When she did, her voice sounded hesitant. "Because you were nice to me at camp."

"Nice? I short-sheeted your bed, remember that?"

"You treated me like a regular person. Nobody treats me that way."

"What about your friends at school?"

"I don't have any."

Dawn started to protest, but just then the door swung open and a frail, rail-thin, elderly woman entered. Her hair was snowy white and pulled back into a bun. She wore a stylish navy blue suit and walked with the aid of a cane.

"Grams," Marlee said, brightening. "This is my friend Dawn—you know, from camp?"

"Emily Hodges," the older woman said while offering a tired-looking smile. Something about her expression warned Dawn that she was upset. She'd seen her own parents' faces wearing the same look.

"Can I go home?" Marlee asked.

"Not yet. Dr. Davis wants to run some more tests."

"But I want to go home."

"I'm having a specialist flown in to check you over," Grandmother Hodges told her. "She'll be here Monday morning."

"But I already have a bunch of doctors."

"This woman is one of the best in her field."

"What's she going to do?"

"Just consult."

"I don't want any more operations."

Grandmother Hodges leaned heavily on her cane. "The doctors make these decisions, not me, dear."

"Grams, please don't let them cut on me anymore." Marlee sounded close to crying.

Grandmother Hodges voice sounded quivery as she said, "Now, now, Marlee...we have to do what the doctors recommend."

"That's why you're having another specialist come in, isn't it? They want to cut on me again! What do they want to take out now? My stomach?"

"Please, dear...I-I can't bear to see you

111

this upset." Marlee's grandmother looked so stricken that Dawn wondered if she should call a nurse.

Marlee must have seen it too, because she hastily said, "It's all right, Grams. Don't get worked up. I'll be okay."

"I'm sorry I can't spend more time with you, dear. I feel poorly still and my doctor wants me in bed today." She reached for the call button. "I'll have one of the nurses come stay with you."

"That's okay. I'll stay with her." The words were out of Dawn's mouth before she could stop them.

Grandmother Hodges turned toward Dawn, as if surprised that she was still in the room. "That's very thoughtful of you. I hate to leave my poor Marlee alone, but I'm not well myself. If I'm feeling better later, I'll come again this evening."

"Don't worry," Dawn insisted. "We'll play some board games, watch some TV. We'll have a good time."

"You wouldn't mind staying?" Marlee asked, her expression both frightened and hopeful.

"I'll just call home and tell my brother to pick me up around 6:00." Silently, she added, *And call Rhonda and let her know*

I won't be at work today.

"I-I'd really like that. You sure it's no problem for you?"

"Nope," Dawn said crossing her fingers behind her back. "No problem at all."

Fourteen

D AWN and Marlee played Monopoly most of the afternoon and Dawn learned more about Marlee Hodges in those few hours than she had during the entire week at camp. She learned that Marlee was smart—into the stratosphere smart. She told Dawn, "They wanted me to skip third and fifth grades, but Grams thought it best that I go ahead and go through fifth grade. What a drag *that* was."

"So you're starting eighth grade this year?"

"Yeah." She named one of the area's most exclusive private schools. "I hope it's better than my old one."

"How?"

"I hope the kids are nicer to me."

"Are you nice to them?"

Marlee jutted her chin. "Of course."

"Come on, be honest."

"Well, I try to be, but everybody's always mean to me."

"Like how?"

"They're just not nice, that's all. Last year, my teacher assigned a group project that I could have done in my sleep and everybody was so *slow* about it. And I got in a big fight with them and then they all hated me." Marlee crossed her arms and flopped back against the pillow. "Nobody understands me."

"I understand you and I don't hate you," Dawn told her.

"You're different."

"No, I'm not. It's just that when a person acts friendly, it's easier to like her."

"Are you saying that I'm unfriendly?"

"Hey, I'm the girl you tried to throw out of her bed at camp, remember? I'd call that pretty unfriendly."

A sheepish smile appeared on Marlee's mouth. "I don't know why I did that," she admitted. "I didn't want to come to camp in the first place, and when I walked in the cabin and saw all those welcome signs and flowers, well...I hated being there even more."

"I know." Dawn's tone turned matter-of-fact. "You were scared, that's all."

"I wasn't scared—I didn't want to go."

Dawn studied Marlee intently. "We're all scared, Marlee. I didn't want to go to camp my first time either. I didn't want to be away from my doctor and my folks. I was afraid I'd get sick and embarrass myself in front of all these strangers. The only reason I went is because my friend Sandy said she'd go."

Marlee wadded the bed linen into her fists, upsetting the Monopoly board. She whispered, "You're right. I *was* scared. Just like I'm scared right now. I don't want any more operations."

"I hope you don't have to have any more."

"Will you keep coming to visit with me until I can go home?"

Marlee's question made Dawn's stomach muscles tighten. She disliked the idea of having to come up to the oncology floor on a regular basis. It made her anxious and nervous to even think about what Marlee was facing. But when she looked at Marlee and saw the fear and loneliness on her face, she reached out and squeezed Marlee's arm and said, "I'll come as often as I can. I promise."

The next day, Dawn breezed into

Marlee's room holding a large brown paper sack. "How's it going?"

Marlee looked pale, but when she saw Dawn, she sat straighter in bed and smiled. "I'm still having trouble keeping food down." She held up her arm with the IV tube running to a plastic bag hanging from the IV stand. "They tell me this stuff's my dinner, but it sure doesn't taste much like hamburgers and milkshakes."

"I know it's a drag, but hang in there." Dawn told her as she looked around the room. There were several large bouquets and baskets on the window sill. Cascades of summer blossoms shimmered in the rays of the afternoon sun. "Wow, I love your flowers."

"The roses are from Grams and the others are from some of her friends." It struck Dawn that there was nothing from Marlee's friends. When she'd been in the hospital, Rhonda had organized a card-writing campaign and she'd been flooded with cards and gifts.

Dawn touched the velvet pink rose petals. "I love roses."

"They're okay." Marlee said.

Dawn turned back to the bed and on the bedside table saw a silver picture frame.

"Hey, it's the camp photo!"

"I had Grams bring it last night."

Dawn picked up the shiny frame, recalling the day by the lake. In the front row, boys were making faces and waving. The familiar grins of the girls in her cabin looked out from one side of the group and far in the back row, she saw Marlee standing stiffly next to Brent. "I thought you hated camp."

"Just at first. I'll, uh, probably go back next year."

"Really?" Dawn gave her a look that was filled with mischief and Marlee blushed. "Maybe we should send out warning letters: 'Beware! Marlee's back.'"

"Don't tease me." But Marlee wore a satisfied grin even as she spoke. "What's in the bag?" she asked, pointing to the sack Dawn still held.

"Oh, nothing much." Dawn felt self-conscious. After seeing all the beautiful flowers, she realized how stupid her gift would probably seem.

"Let me see." Marlee looked animated as she grabbed the sack and opened it up. She reached inside and pulled out Mr. Ruggers. "Hey, it's your teddy bear."

Dawn felt her neck and cheeks grow

warm with color. "I know he's scruffy-looking, but he's a good friend. He went through everything with me—my first stay in the hospital, my transplant. I just thought you might like to have him around." She added hastily, "It's all right if you don't. You won't hurt my feelings if you don't want me to leave him."

"You'd let me keep him?"

"Just until you go home. And only if you really want to keep him."

"Thanks," she answered with a smile. "I'd love to have him with me." Marlee tried to straighten his permanently flopped ear. "I'll keep him here in bed with me."

They watched a sappy movie on TV and played cards. When Grandmother Hodges arrived after supper, Dawn went to the lobby to wait for Rob to come get her. Dawn worked extra hours at the ice cream parlor Monday afternoon and listened to Rhonda scold her for skipping out on Saturday.

"My uncle was steamed, but I covered for you," Rhonda insisted. Dawn thanked her and kept busy, grateful for the activity. It kept her mind off of Marlee and the upcoming consultation with the new doctor.

When she arrived that evening, Marlee was sitting up in bed, sorting through a stack of novels. "Come in," Marlee cried with a smile that lit up her thin face.

"You must have had good news."

"The best. Dr. Dillard—the special one Grams had brought in on my case—reviewed all my X-rays and tests today. And guess what?"

"You're really made of cotton candy inside?"

"No, silly. I don't have to have any more operations!"

"Oh, Marlee, that's super news! So does that mean you can go home?"

A frown formed on Marlee's forehead. "No. That's the only part that's not good."

The information puzzled Dawn too. "Why can't you leave?"

"Dr. Dillard says that there's a tumor on my stomach. But since I've already had two operations, she won't operate again. Honestly, Dawn," Marlee said, leaning forward as if delivering gossip, "surgery is a drag. It takes forever to get over it."

"So, no surgery, So now what?"

Marlee flopped back against her pillow. "The usual—radiation."

"No chemo?"

"Not this time."

"Then what's *that* machine doing?"

120

Dawn pointed to a small mechanical box on a cart parked beside Marlee's bed. A line ran from it to a vein in her arm.

"That's a morphine infusion pump," explained Marlee. "It's for the pain. When it gets really bad, I can adjust this control—" she pointed, "and presto—instant relief. Boy! Does it ever work." She rolled her eyes. "I feel good enough to go off the high dive."

"I could never feel *that* good," Dawn kidded and they both laughed.

"So you'll be here for awhile," Dawn stated.

"I guess. They're just going to be rolling me down to radiology a couple times a week to shrink this thing. And once it's shrunk, then I can go home."

"Is that what they told you?"

"Not exactly."

For some reason, Dawn felt a coldness creeping up her spine. "Well, what exactly did they tell you?"

"Just about the radiation. I figured the rest out by myself."

"But for right now, you're just a guest of the hospital?"

Marlee sighed and made a face. "Yeah. Much as I don't want to be. Besides, it's easier on Grams this way. But you'll keep coming to visit me, won't you?"

Marlee looked so eager and hopeful that Dawn didn't have the heart to tell her no. "I'll play you a game of Monopoly," Dawn said dragging a chair over.

While Marlee arranged the game board, Dawn thought about all that Marlee had told her. She wasn't positive she understood the business about "just radiation" for Marlee's cancer. She made a mental note to have a talk with Katie. If anyone could explain it to her, Katie could.

Fifteen

WHEN Rob brought Katie to the house for dinner two nights later, Dawn asked her about Marlee's treatment. She, Katie and Rob were outside in the backyard gazebo eating watermelon, after Mrs. Rochelle had insisted that she and Mr. Rochelle could clean up the kitchen. As the three of them watched the sunset, Dawn broached the subject. "I'm just not clear on why a doctor wouldn't operate on a tumor," she said.

Katie didn't answer right away. Dawn studied her for some hint of what she was thinking, but her expression was impassive. Finally Katie said, "Honey, I really can't discuss the specifics of any case with you. It isn't ethical."

"Well, forget it's Marlee. Let's just say it's anybody. Why not operate?"

123

Katie sighed. "There are lots of reasons doctors make the choices they do. Surgery is always risky. No doctor should put a patient through it unnecessarily."

"But she—I mean, suppose a patient—has already been through it twice. Why not again?" Dawn asked.

"Sometimes chemo and radiation can do the trick."

"Marlee's had both before. Now, a tumor's back. I remember when I had a relapse, the doctors suggested a bone marrow transplant."

"You had a different type of cancer. A marrow transplant is effective in treating leukemia, but not others."

Dawn felt she wasn't getting any real answers. Exasperated, she blurted, "Is Marlee going to get well?"

Katie set her slice of watermelon onto the wooden steps and wiped her hands on her napkin. "I thought this was supposed to be a general conversation, and not about Marlee's case in particular?"

"You two aren't arguing, are you?" Rob asked, glancing from one to the other. "I couldn't stand having my two favorite women fighting with each other."

Instantly, Dawn felt ashamed. "I'm

sorry, Katie."

"Oh, Dawn, I'm sorry too—sorry that I can't tell you what you want to hear."

Even though it was difficult to make out Katie's features in the gathering twilight, Dawn could sense the tension and uneasiness in her voice and posture. "I shouldn't have pressed you. But how can I find out? Who will talk to me?"

Katie sighed. "Marlee's grandmother is the only one, really, at liberty to discuss Marlee. It's up to her."

"But I hardly know her."

Katie reached over and flipped Dawn's hair on her shoulder in a gesture of tenderness. "I wish I could be more of a help to you, honey, but I can't. I just can't."

*   *   *   *   *

"Dawn? Is that you? What's up?"

She'd spent an hour deciding whether or not to call Brent. Now that she heard his voice on the phone, she felt a rush of relief. "I-I hope I'm not interrupting anything."

"Never. I was under my car trying to fix something that's leaking." He paused. "Are you all right?"

"Oh, sure. I'm fine." She sat on her bed.

The lamp on her bedside table cast a warm yellow glow over the new bedspread she'd bought for herself.

"So you just called to hear my voice?" His familiar southern drawl made her feel relaxed and calmer.

"It's not me—it's Marlee."

"I got your letter saying she was in the hospital. Has something happened?"

"I'm not sure," Dawn twisted the phone cord around her finger. "She's still in the hospital, but I'm not sure what's going on." She let her frustration and concern spill out in a flood of words. "I just wish I had been able to sit in on the consultation with the specialist, then maybe I could understand things better."

"Why?" He asked. "Why do you want to know?"

For a moment, she couldn't answer. Why *did* she want to know? What business *was* it of hers? "I guess because she's my friend."

"You were her camp counselor and you felt sorry for her and you showed her a good time in spite of herself. But I never remember you telling me Marlee was your friend. Have you two gotten real close since she's been in the hospital?"

Brent was asking a hard question and she was at a loss to answer it. Rhonda was her friend and there were others from school. Where did Marlee fit into her life?

"I have lots of friends," Dawn blurted. "Can't I have lots of friends?"

"There's nothing wrong with having friends," Brent said cheerfully. "I was just asking if something had changed between you and Marlee."

"I understand her better now." She told him some of Marlee's background. "I mean, can you imagine being the only kid in a house with a really sick grandmother all your life? She grew up awfully lonesome. She's never made friends easily. And now...well now, it doesn't seem like a whole lot's being done about her cancer."

Dawn felt her voice grow quivery, but she continued, "When I found out about my relapse, I got to be a part of deciding about the bone marrow transplant. All they're doing for Marlee is some radiation and pumping her full of morphine."

"Is that bad?" Brent wanted to know.

"It just seems weird to me. If all they're going to do is radiate her, she could do it on an outpatient basis. Why does she have to stay in the hospital?"

"If her grandmother's old and sick, maybe she can't take care of her at home."

Brent's simple observation made sense and she wondered why she hadn't thought of it. "Could that be all there is to it?"

"You can't second-guess her doctors," Brent said. "If you really want to know, you'll have to talk to her grandmother."

"Maybe I'll have to." They talked a few more minutes, and Dawn hung up with a promise to keep him informed. She paced the floor of her room. It was late, but she wasn't sleepy. Questions and emotions kept whirling through her like a summer storm.

Why was she so entangled in Marlee's illness? Especially when she'd once told Rob that she didn't want friends who had cancer. But Brent was right. Marlee and she weren't really and truly friends. Sandy had been her friend. Her *best* friend. The unbidden memory of Brent's sister sneaked into her mind. *Go away!* she told the image. She didn't want to think about Sandy now. She warted to figure out what to do about Marlee.

Dawn finally fell into an exhausted slumber without one of her questions answered and without any of her ragged emotions settled.

*   *   *   *   *

Dawn got her chance to talk to Marlee's grandmother the very next afternoon. She got off the elevator on the oncology floor and was walking past the activity room when she saw the elderly woman sitting in a lounge chair inside the empty room.

With her heart thudding, Dawn entered. Grandmother Hodges was laying back in the chair, her feet elevated, her eyes closed. Unsure if she were asleep, Dawn softly cleared her throat. The older woman's eyes opened and Dawn could tell she'd been crying. "I-I hope I didn't disturb you," she said.

Grandmother Hodges studied Dawn as if trying to bring her into focus. "Oh, yes," she said. "You're Marlee's friend."

"Yes, ma'am. I was on my way to visit her. How is she today?"

"Sleeping. It's the pain medication, you know. It makes her comfortable enough to sleep."

Dawn felt her mouth go dry. There was so much she wanted to ask, but didn't know how. "Umm, she told me the specialist wasn't going to operate."

"No. They won't be operating again," answered the woman.

Dawn felt her knees tremble and her fingertips turn icy cold. "Mrs. Hodges, will you please tell me something? I've tried to get the answer from other people, but no one will tell me the truth."

Grandmother Hodges's face became a solemn mask. "You want to know if Marlee's going to get well, don't you?"

"Yes, ma'am. She really wants to go home."

Grandmother Hodges sighed. Then she answered softly, "No, my dear. She won't be going home. My poor baby is dying. She's dying."

Sixteen

D AWN felt numb all over. She thought about screaming. She thought about running away. She thought about collapsing. But all she was able to do was stand, rock solid still, rooted to the floor. She wasn't surprised about Marlee, not really. She realized that deep down, she'd known the truth all along.

"Does Marlee know?" she asked Grandmother Hodges, who had begun to cry softly.

"No." The old woman grabbed Dawn's hand. "You won't tell her, will you?" she begged. "Please say you'll keep it a secret."

"She'll be able to figure it out. I know she will."

"I want her to have her illusions as long as possible."

Dawn thought Marlee should be told.

She'd want to know if it were her. She shuddered as she thought back to how sick she'd been after her transplant and how tired she'd felt. Even the act of breathing had been a chore. If it hadn't been for Rob urging her on, she didn't think she would have made it.

She asked, "Do Marlee's doctors have any idea how long she has?"

"Evidently, there are tumors all inside her body pressing against her vital organs." Grandmother Hodges' voice caught. "It won't be long."

Knowing the truth and *hearing* the truth were two separate things, Dawn decided. "I was on my way to see her." Her lips felt wooden as she said the words.

"She loves having you visit her. Every evening she tells me about what the two of you did and she tells me how she can't wait to see you the next day."

"Doesn't anybody else come visit her?"

The elderly woman shook her head. "There's no one else. I'm all she has and she's all I have." Her eyes filled with tears and she fished a linen handkerchief from her lap. "Please excuse me."

Dawn watched her weep softly. "I should go in and see her now." Still overcome,

Grandmother Hodges nodded. Dawn slipped out of the room and headed down the hall. She forced herself not to cry. It wouldn't be good to go into Marlee's room crying. As she passed the nurse's station, Katie caught her eye.

Quickly, Katie came around the desk and took Dawn's arm. "You're pale as a ghost. Are you all right?"

"I just talked with Marlee's grandmother." Katie nodded and Dawn added, "She told me everything."

"I'm sorry I couldn't say anything the other night."

"It's okay—really."

Katie gave her a quick hug. "You're a very special person, Dawn. I'm so glad I know you."

Dawn hugged her back. "You too."

Dawn put a smile on her face and swung into Marlee's room. "Ready for a game of Monopoly? This time, *I* get to be the banker."

Marlee was propped up. Her skin had a yellowish cast and her face looked pinched with pain. "It's about time you came," she said crossly.

Ignoring her tone of voice, Dawn asked, "Are you okay?"

"I hurt."

Dawn motioned toward the morphine pump. "Isn't it working?"

"I'm trying not to use it so much."

"Why not? You should—it helps you."

"It makes me groggy and sleepy. I hate sleeping so much." Marlee shifted in bed and grimaced. "Will you open my blinds? I want to see the sunlight. Grams always closes them and I hate lying here in the dark."

Dawn opened them and immediately the room was filled with a wash of summer morning light. "Is that better?"

"Yes." Marlee did appear more relaxed, so Dawn brought her favorite chair over to the bed. "I don't feel like playing a game," Marlee confessed.

"What do you want to do?"

"I hate it here. I want to go home."

"But you can't leave today."

Marlee turned her body toward Dawn, and winced. Dawn clenched her fists, but otherwise tried not to react to the pain. "I don't like the way they treat me here."

"How's that?"

"They're keeping secrets from me."

Dawn's heart gave a little lurch. "Oh, I don't think—"

"Yes, they are. I can tell. Grams is always whispering to the nurses. And my doctors hardly visit anymore. They've even stopped taking me down to radiology."

"Marlee, after you first got admitted, you were complaining about *too* much medicine and *too* many visits."

"It's different now."

Agitated, Dawn got up and walked to the window. Staring out at the bright blue sky, the memory of Sandy stole over her. Sandy who always knew what to say. Who always knew how to be kind and understanding. If only Sandy were here now.

Silently Dawn pleaded, *Let me say the right things to Marlee. Please let me say the right things.* She turned back toward the bed, resting her weight against the sill. "This is a big hospital, Marlee," she said. "You're not the only sick person here, you know."

"You think I'm terrible for complaining, don't you?"

Marlee's voice sounded so small and miserable that Dawn hurried to her bedside and took her hand. "Of course I don't."

"Do you like me, Dawn?"

"Like you?"

"Are we friends? I-I want you to be my

friend."

"Why would I come here all the time if we weren't friends?"

"I guess you wouldn't." Evidently, another spasm of pain went through Marlee, because she gave a slight cry.

"Don't try and be brave," Dawn urged, her insides feeling like twisted knots. "Friends can't stand to see their friends hurting."

Marlee reached over and adjusted a knob on the morphine pump. Moments later, the look of pain eased on her face. Her ragged breathing became more even and her body relaxed on the bed. With eyes closed, she said, "I'm such a loser."

"Why do you say that?"

"I never fit in any place. Not at school, not at camp, not at home."

"But your grandmother loves you very much. I can tell."

"I know she does. I hardly remember my parents. Mostly in the pictures Grams has of them. Sometimes I wish I had a mother to be with me. Grams and I did all right together, but still...." Marlee's eye closed, and for a moment Dawn wondered if she'd drifted off to sleep. "Poor Grams. If only I hadn't gotten sick. Why'd I have to get sick, Dawn?" Marlee asked in a whisper.

Unshed tears clogged Dawn's throat. Why didn't she have any answers? "It's not your fault, Marlee. Nobody gets to pick what happens to them in life. Things just *happen*. We have to keep going on, no matter what happens."

"This stuff is making me tired," Marlee said, motioning toward the pump. "Will you stay with me until I go to sleep?"

"I'll stay," Dawn told her.

"I will get to go home, won't I, Dawn?" Marlee's voice faded off and she fell asleep. Dawn slowly extracted her hand from Marlee's fragile grasp. She was grateful that she hadn't had to answer. Dawn knew she couldn't have lied to the girl about her going home. She sat for a long time beside Marlee's bed and watched her sleep. Later, when she was certain Marlee wouldn't awaken, she left the room to call Rob to come and take her home.

Seventeen

"**T**HIS will be my last day on the job."
Dawn tied her apron behind her
back as she made her announcement to
Rhonda.

"What! You can't be serious." Rhonda
dropped the ice cream scoop she was
washing in the sink with a loud clank.

"I've already called your uncle and told
him."

"But you said you loved this job."

"I do."

"Then why?"

"I have to quit. Marlee's dying," Dawn
told her, expecting the phrase to explain
everything.

But an uncomprehending look crossed
Rhonda's face. "What's that got to do with
you?"

"Because she needs me to be with her.

She *wants* me to be with her."

"But what about all the plans we've made? Buying new school clothes? What about all the fun we're having?"

Dawn stared at Rhonda in amazement. "Didn't you hear me? I said Marlee's *dying*."

Rhonda turned and began to furiously wash the sink full of ice cream scoops. "Well, I think it's weird and creepy to hang around someone who's dying."

"It isn't weird or creepy," Dawn declared. "It's something I have to do."

"How long?"

"'How long' what?"

"How long will you be with her?"

"However long it takes." Dawn felt bewildered by Rhonda's response, by her lack of sensitivity. She whipped around, grabbed a damp sponge and hurried over to wipe off table tops in the empty shop. *This is ridiculous*, she kept telling herself. How could Rhonda be so heartless?

Dawn heard the sound of crying coming from behind the counter. She dropped the sponge and ran back to the sink. Rhonda was leaning over the basin of water, tears slipping down her cheeks. "What's wrong?" Dawn asked.

Rhonda burst into sobs and grabbed Dawn and hugged her fiercely. Shocked by her outburst, Dawn cautiously patted her on the back. "Why are you crying?"

"I don't want you to go away," Rhonda said, gulping for air.

"I'm not going anywhere," Dawn insisted, confused. "I'm just quitting my job, that's all."

"But you'll start school with me?"

"Of course, I'll be starting school. Why wouldn't I?"

"You're not going to get sick ever again, are you?"

Was that what was bothering Rhonda? That *she* might get sick? That *she* might die? "It's not in my plans."

Rhonda wiped the back of her hand over her cheeks. Melted chocolate made a dark smear on her skin. Dawn reached over and dabbed at it with a paper towel. "You've got fudge on your face," she explained. "There, I've got it off."

"How will I manage without you?" Rhonda asked with a self-conscious half-laugh. "If you aren't here, who's going to look out for me? Who's going to tell me I'm making an idiot of myself over some cute guy?"

"I'll hang around and keep an eye on you."

"How long will you hang around with me?"

Dawn held onto Rhonda's shoulder and looked her straight in the eye. "Until we're both old and fat and wrinkled."

"Promise?"

"Promise."

*   *   *   *   *

Dawn lay awake in the dark. The lighted digits on her radio alarm clock read 5:00 A.M. *Go back to sleep*, she told herself. *You've got to be at the hospital in a few hours and you'll be all tired out if you don't.* She didn't want to fall asleep while visiting Marlee. But no amount of plumping up her pillow or snuggling down under her covers could make sleep come.

Her mind kept resisting what her heart kept telling her to go do. *I can't*, she said inwardly. *Yes, you can. You must*, another inward voice directed. In the end, the "must" voice won out. Quietly, she slipped from her bed, tugged on her summer robe and stole into the hallway.

The house was quiet, her parents and Rob still asleep. A nightlight from the bathroom cast a glow along the wall. She followed it and at the end of the hall she found the door to the attic. Beside the door was the flashlight her father always kept plugged into the wall socket. She took it, turned it on and slowly climbed the stairs. At the top, inside the attic, she swung the light in a wide arc, throwing beams into the dark corners.

In a few hours, the summer sun would make the area unbearably hot. But right now, the room was only stuffy, a contrast from the air-conditioned coolness of the house below. "Where is it?" she asked aloud, swinging the flashlight in a circle. Where had she put it?

The light beams fell on an old dresser. Behind it, there was a set of wooden shelves. Her heart hammered as the rays of light fell across an old, dog-eared box. Forcing the dresser quietly aside, she tugged the box off the shelf. Clutching it, she dumped a pile of old curtains from a sagging overstuffed chair, sat down and placed the box in her lap.

Dust had settled on the lid and she blew on it, making it billow. She rested the flashlight on the arm of the chair so that it spread a circle of light across her lap.

Open it, she told herself. It should be so simple. But her hands were shaking and her mouth was dry and every nerve in her body tingled. "Nothing's hard about taking a lid off a box," she whispered aloud as if the words would give her courage.

The smells of the attic clung to her. She wanted go back downstairs and wash the grime off her hands and climb back into bed. But instead she lifted the lid. Inside the box everything was exactly as she remembered. All that remained of Sandy Chandler's life lay cradled in her lap. At least, all that remained of the things she could touch and smell and see.

She had expected to break down, fall apart, as she'd done so often in the past. But although a huge lump had risen to her throat, she didn't cry. Instead, a feeling of warmth and tenderness spread through her. Her finger caressed the hair combs and popcorn necklace. Each memento was like a tiny sparkling jewel that glowed in her memory.

She untied the bundle of letters and re-read them, one by one, from the first, following Sandy's return home from the hospital where they'd met, to the last, postmarked from Mexico. Sandy had written, *Good night, my friend. Go with God,* in small, neat, perfect handwriting.

At the very bottom of the box, in a plain white envelope, she discovered the page from the Bible, Ecclesiastes 3. She didn't have to read it. She knew the words by heart. Aloud, she said, "'For everything there is a season...A time to live and a time to die.'"

Dawn sighed and rested her head against the chair. "I miss you, Sandy," she said. "I wish I could talk to you. Tell you about camp. And Brent." She smiled. "He's pretty cute and he kisses real nice. Of course with my limited experience, I'm no expert."

There was a window high above her, at the highest point of the attic. Daylight was breaking and she could see pale streaks of pink in the sky. Soon, it would be time to get ready to go to the hospital. "I wish I could tell you about Marlee too, Sandy. She's kind of a pain, but I like her anyway." Dawn said in the close air. "I wish you could have been a CIT with me this summer." She thought about the fun they might have had and smiled again.

Dawn stared absently into space, images of the two of them running through her mind's eye like a scene from a movie. The pretty pictures made her feel warm and soft. Yet, they always ended with the image of her standing alone by her front door, receiving a box from the mailman. *Alone.* That's how her memories of her with Sandy always ended.

She closed her eyes and saw herself walking down a road. Sandy was walking with her, but then somewhere along the way, Sandy dropped back. She saw herself stop and turn and signal to her friend to come beside her, but Sandy simply stood and waved. And no matter how urgently Dawn beckoned to her, Sandy would not come.

Slowly Dawn opened her eyes. She was in her attic and day was breaking outside the window. She thought of Marlee. Soon she too, would slip away from her. Why did the people she cared about go off and leave her?

Dawn stood, her eyes still fixed on the outside sky, growing brighter each minute. From below, she heard the sounds of water running. Her father taking his morning shower. Life was going on all around her. *Her life.* She put what was left of Sandy Chandler's away in the box and took it downstairs to her room.

Eighteen

DAWN sensed a hushed atmosphere on the oncology floor the moment she got off the elevator. The first person she saw was Marlee's grandmother, shuffling down the hall with her cane. Dawn hurried up beside her, her heart thudding. "Is everything all right?" Dawn asked.

"Yes. Marlee's resting. I'm going down to the lounge to prop up my feet. Doctor's orders."

Dawn tagged after her, unsure of what else to do. She watched the elderly woman settle into the chair and elevate the foot rest. "Can I get you something?" she asked.

"No thank you, dear. The nurses have taken good care of me." She gazed at Dawn with kind, tired eyes. "I want to thank you for being here for Marlee these past six weeks. It's meant so much to her to have

146

somebody more her age care about her."

"You mean a lot to her too."

The old woman smiled wanly. "Marlee and I make an odd couple, don't we?" she asked. "How I remember that first day she came to live with me. My son and daughter-in-law had been killed in a car crash." Her eyes grew misty. "You see, there was no one else but me to take little Marlee. She was so scared and confused and she missed her mama so much at first."

"It must have been hard for both of you."

"I gave her everything I could, but I know she didn't have a normal childhood. How could she? I was 67 years old when she came into my life. With a heart condition." She shook her head, as if confused by life's events.

"And then when they told me she had cancer—I could hardly believe it. How often I've wished it could have been me instead of Marlee. I mean, she has her whole life in front of her. And me? Well, I'm an old woman who has buried a husband and my only child. No one expects to bury her child, much less her grandchild...." She let her sentence trail off. Finally, she added, "I plan to ask the good Lord some things when I see him."

Dawn felt at a loss for something to say. Inside, her heart was breaking. To her, nothing made any sense. The old lived; the young died. Where did she fit in? Grandmother Hodges' eyes closed and Dawn stole from the room, walking quickly toward the room where Marlee lay.

Dawn entered Marlee's room, stood by her bed and stared down at her. She watched her chest rise and fall. Every breath sounded shallow and rapid. Dawn touched Marlee's hand and had almost decided to return later, when suddenly Marlee's good eye opened. She whispered, "Hi, Dawn."

"Hi yourself."

"I was having a wonderful dream."

"I'm sorry I woke you."

"Brent was in it." Dawn saw slight color spread across Marlee's cheeks. "Do you ever hear from him?"

"He calls me and he writes. He asks about you."

"About me?"

"He thought you were a wonderful diver."

A soft smile played with Marlee's mouth. "Did he ever kiss you?"

Now it was Dawn's turn to smile. "Yes, he did."

"Was it wonderful?"

"Didn't we have this discussion at camp with the other girls?"

"I just listened that time. I didn't have any good stories to tell like Cindy did." Marlee's eye closed and for a moment Dawn thought she'd fallen back to sleep. But then she said weakly, "I wished I could have been kissed, just once. For real. Not like in my dream."

A fist-sized lump stuck in Dawn's throat. She remembered how, in her diary, Sandy had written, *Mike kissed me tonight...I can't wait until next summer. Then Mike and I can practice some more.*

"You don't mind me dreaming about Brent kissing me, do you?"

"I don't mind."

"Will you see him at camp next summer?"

Dawn didn't have the heart to tell her that she wouldn't be returning to camp. She couldn't go back again with both Sandy and Marlee gone. It would hurt too much. "Lots can happen before next summer," Dawn said.

Marlee tried to twist beneath the covers. "Where's Mr. Ruggers?" Dawn fumbled at the head of the bed for the teddy bear.

She placed him in Marlee's arms and Marlee rubbed his well-worn fur against her cheek. "You'll have to give him a bath," she said. "He smells like the hospital."

"He wants to stay here with you."

"I'm tired, Dawn." Marlee's voice was so soft, Dawn had to lean down to hear her.

Something cold settled in Dawn's stomach. She'd said the same thing herself, to Rob just before her heart had stopped beating after her transplant procedure. She remembered well that feeling of unbearable weariness. "I know you are."

"Will you do me a favor?" Marlee asked.

"What can I do?"

"Don't let Grams know that I'm never going home again. I know she's going to miss me and I hate to see her cry."

Dawn couldn't speak. It hurt too much. Both Marlee and her grandmother wanted to shield each other from the truth. Dawn managed to say, "Sure. It'll be our secret."

"I'm scared, Dawn. What's waiting for me?" Marlee's voice was barely a whisper.

"Maybe another dream about Brent," she offered, trying to quiet Marlee's fears.

"Where will I be if I don't wake up here?"

Dawn longed for something to say, something to bring Marlee comfort. Dawn smoothed Marlee's forehead. Her skin had grown cool and dry. "I had a friend named Sandy—remember?"

"Yes...the girl who died."

"She was Brent's sister."

Dawn saw Marlee's facial muscles work as she tried to process the information. "Is that why you liked each other?"

"Maybe." Dawn laced Marlee's fingers through hers as she continued. "Sandy's in heaven. She left me some of her favorite things. And she let me know that's where she went. She's exactly your age, Marlee, and I believe she'll be waiting for you when you get there."

The frown lines smoothed out on Marlee's face. "Do you think she'll like me? Not many girls like me. You're the only real friend I've ever had."

Tears had pooled in Dawn's eyes until Marlee's face shimmered and squiggled, making it impossible for Dawn to see her clearly. "Sandy will be your friend too," she whispered.

"Are you sure?"

"She liked everybody, and they liked her. I know she'll be your friend too. You tell her hi for me, all right?"

Marlee nodded and pulled Mr. Ruggers into the hollow of her neck. "I'll tell her," she promised. "And you tell Brent hi from me."

Dawn watched Marlee's eyelids close as she drifted off to sleep. Before leaving, she pulled the covers up around Marlee's thin shoulders and made certain Mr. Ruggers was touching her cheek. She told Katie at the nursing station that she'd be back later.

But that morning turned out to be the last time that Dawn ever spoke to Marlee Hodges. That night, Marlee slipped into a coma. Two days later, while her grandmother held her hand, she died.

Katie called Dawn at home to tell her. Dawn called Brent and told him. Then she crawled beneath her covers and sobbed.

Nineteen

M ARLEE was buried on a hot August morning. The cornflower-blue sky was decorated with puffy white clouds that looked like wads of colorless cotton candy. Dawn had cried so much before the funeral that she made it through the service fairly dry-eyed. Rob and Katie went with her and it helped having them by her side.

Dawn stared at the mantel of pale pink roses draped over Marlee's coffin. The minister's words drifted in and out of her consciousness. "Ashes to ashes, dust to dust," he said. Dawn felt dull and listless, like burned-up ashes.

"He shall wipe away every tear and turn our mourning into joy," Dawn heard the man say. She wondered if she'd ever feel joyous again. She let her gaze drift away from the coffin to the green, lush lawn of the cemetery, broken by colorful patches of flowers placed in vases beside bronze plaques. Row upon row they stretched, as far as her eye could see.

She felt Rob put his arm around her shoulder. "It's over," he told her gently. She nodded. As they started across the emerald green grass, Dawn heard someone call her name and turned to see Grandmother Hodges and her chauffeur coming toward her. Dawn met the old woman half-way.

They hugged. Grandmother Hodges was dressed in black and she felt feather-light in Dawn's arms. Her voice wavered as she said, "Thank you for coming, my dear. Marlee wanted to make sure I gave you this."

Leaning on her cane, she turned toward her chauffeur, who handed Dawn a small, but elegant shopping bag. Inside was Mr. Ruggers and a little box wrapped with a red ribbon. "Thank you," Dawn said, fingering the floppy-eared bear.

"Marlee loved that bear of yours. Funny—she had a whole room full of beautiful dolls and stuffed animals I'd given her over the years. But none of them meant as much to her as your bear."

Dawn felt tears mist over her eyes. "He has a way of growing on you."

"Thank you again for all you did for Marlee. She loved you like a sister."

Dawn's chest felt heavy, as if her heart might break. "She was like a sister to me too."

"I'm feeling rather poorly," Grandmother Hodges apologized." But if you'd ever like to talk, please call me."

Dawn promised she would. Marlee's grandmother leaned into her chauffeur, who led her toward the long black limousine waiting on the roadside.

"You okay, Squirt?" Rob asked. His term of endearment sounded out of place to Dawn. She was too old for childish nicknames anymore. "Let's go home," he said, gently directing her toward his car.

"In a minute," she told him. "I'd like to be alone, if that's okay."

He took Katie's hand. "We'll wait right here. Take all the time you need."

Clutching the bag, Dawn walked aimlessly amid the plaques and headstones. When she was some distance away, she opened the sack and gazed at the bear. "So, what do you think, Mr. Ruggers? It looks like it's just me and you again."

She thought of the time she'd grown tired of fighting for her life and had insisted Rob take the bear. "You're like a boomerang," she told the stuffed animal. "You keep coming back. But I'm glad to see you again. And thanks for making Marlee happy. You're a good ol' bear." Her voice caught and tears swam in her eyes.

"Why do you suppose I'm always the one left behind, Mr. Ruggers? Why am I always the one who has to keep saying goodbye to my friends?"

The bear stared at her through his one glassy eye, reminding her for all the world of Marlee and her moment at camp when a hundred glass marbles had bounced on the assembly hall floor. The image made Dawn smile softly. She pulled out the ribbon-wrapped box. A note was attached in Marlee's handwriting. It read:

Dawn,

Since I won't be around next summer, I have to count on my "sister" to carry on for me. Please keep on being nice to us campers, even if some girl acts like a brat. You were right. I was scared. But I'm not scared anymore. I'll tell Sandy hi when I meet her.

The writing squiggled as tears slid down her cheeks. Carefully, she untied the ribbon. Inside the box lay a pile of gray ashes. Gingerly, Dawn sifted them with her thumb and forefinger. The silt settled on her skin, and somehow, also on her heart. All at once, she knew that she had no choice. She'd have to go back to camp. She'd have to return the ashes to the bonfire next summer. For Marlee. For Sandy. They were all sisters. Linked by the bond of cancer, bound by the thread of hope.

Dawn lifted her fingers, staring in fascination at the way the gray ashes clung. Gently, she puffed and watched the fine silt drift skyward. *Dust in the wind.* She saw then that they were *all* dust in the wind, until they each became jewels in a crown of life.

And she realized that some of them— like herself—were allowed to go on living for all the ones who couldn't. *Life is a gift.* A tingling feeling stole over her as she understood that she, Dawn Rochelle, had been chosen to continue on. Day by day. Month by month. Year by year.

Dawn kept looking up. She was no longer able to see the tiny particles of ashes. Yet she was *certain* that they were there, floating off in the summer breeze high above the earth.

Dawn closed the box, hugged her stuffed bear tightly and, feeling the hot, delicious warmth of the sun soaking through her dress, whispered, "Come on, Mr. Ruggers. It's time to go home."